FOR LOVE OF ELI

This Large Print Book carries the Seal of Approval of N.A.V.H.

QUILTS OF LOVE SERIES

FOR LOVE OF ELI

LOREE LOUGH

THORNDIKE PRESS

A part of Gale, Cengage Learning

Detroit • New York • San Francisco • New Haven, Conn • Waterville, Maine • London

Copyright © 2013 Loree Lough.
Scripture quotations from the Common English Bible, Copyright © 2011 by the Common English Bible. All rights reserved. Used by permission.
Thorndike Press, a part of Gale, Cengage Learning.

LIBRARY OF CONGRESS CATALOGING-IN-PUBLICATION DATA

Lough, Loree.
   For love of Eli / by Loree Lough. — Large print edition.
     pages ; cm. — (Thorndike Press large print clean reads) (Quilts of love series)
   ISBN 978-1-4104-6270-1 (hardcover) — ISBN 1-4104-6270-6 (hardcover)
  1. Orphans—Fiction. 2. Quiltmakers—Fiction. 3. Memories—Fiction.
  4. Heirlooms—Fiction. 5. Large type books. I. Title.
PS3562.O8147F67 2013b
813'.6—dc23   2013027114

Published in 2013 by arrangement with Abingdon Press

Printed in the United States of America
1 2 3 4 5 6 7 17 16 15 14 13

To Larry, love of my life, keeper of my heart, my best friend and lifelong companion; to my beloved mom, now living in Paradise, whose fondness for words — those read and those written — helped inspire my own relationship with the craft (I will miss you, always!); and of course, to my Lord and Savior.

ACKNOWLEDGMENTS

I'd like to acknowledge my cousin Dawn, whose artistry with squares of fabric, thread, and needles is rivaled only by the works of Van Gogh, Botticelli, Mantegna, and other great masters; her help in designing Eli's quilt was as fascinating as it was educational (and I'll tell you so in person at the next Lough reunion)!

To my cousin Maureen and her daughter, Gina, for loaning me their names and personalities, which added fun and quirky characters to the story.

I'd also like to acknowledge all the people in the Blacksburg, Virginia, area who helped me find cool and interesting places to "put" the characters, and to that oh-so-friendly Virginia trooper who helped me with mapping strategies!

Last, but certainly not least, my most humble gratitude to God, for blessing me with the ideas, the words, the time, and the energy that made this story possible.

Hello, dear readers!

I'm so glad and grateful that of all the books you could have chosen, you picked *For Love of Eli* to keep you company today! The quilt featured in this story is called a "memory quilt," with good reason: Our lovely heroine, Taylor, designed this one to help her orphaned nephew remember his mom and dad by sewing bits of their history into the story of their lives. For this is a story about memories and how they affect us.

But before you dig in, let me share the story that helped inspire this novel.

A while ago, on my way to a friend's house for an impromptu dinner, I spent forty punishing minutes in bumper-to-bumper traffic. I'd barely escaped the gridlock when a dreaded *thump-whump* told me I had a flat tire. Fifteen greasy, sweaty minutes later, I was back on the road. "Better find a shortcut," I muttered, "if you don't want to be late." (And anyone who knows me understands that tardiness is a big no-no in my book.) So, I typed my friend's address into my trusty GPS, and it led me through parts of the city that I never knew existed. Somehow, I arrived right on time, and spent the first few minutes entertaining my friend with my "How I Got to Your House" tale.

Imagine my surprise when she blamed *herself* for my wild goose chase: If she'd given me a little more notice, I might have avoided the traffic jam. She should have invited me on a weekend and spared me the whole GPS escapade. And the flat tire? Well, she could have spared me that, too (pun intended), by suggesting that we get together at my house instead of making me travel all the way across town.

But I can't be too hard on her because, like most humans, I've done the same thing. Aren't we an odd bunch, taking ourselves to task for things we couldn't possibly have predicted, prevented, or controlled? It's as if we think we were born with godly powers, the way we sometimes carry on!

Reece Montgomery, the hero in *For Love of Eli,* wasted *years* beating himself up for things over which he had no control: he convinced himself that he should have noticed that his sister's depression — sparked by the death of her young husband — had gone far above and beyond the normal grieving process. And he believed that if he hadn't assumed Margo was asleep on that awful, life-changing night, he never would have left her alone. If he'd been in the house instead of out picking up a pizza, he could have stopped her from driving to the pharmacy.

As so many of us do when grief threatens our sanity, Reece needed someone with whom to share his self-imposed guilt. First, he blamed his sister's husband, because if Eliot had kept his promise to Margo — instead of volunteering for another tour of duty in Afghanistan — he wouldn't have died in a fiery IED explosion. And Reece shared his blame with the story's heroine, for no reason other than Taylor Bradley reminded him of her brother, Eliot.

It'll take a lot of prayer if Reece is to find his way back to God, the inventor of mercy and forgiveness. Will he ask the Almighty's help in letting up on himself — *and on Taylor* — before it's too late?

My prayer for *you,* dear reader, is that the Father will help you discern between the things you *should* take responsibility for and those that are totally out of your control, and that when you face those out-of-your-control moments, He'll fill you with the strength you'll need to bear up under it . . . plus an ounce more!

I hope you'll write me to share what you liked best about *For Love of Eli* (I answer every letter, you know!) c/o Abingdon Press, P. O. Box 801, Nashville, TN 37202, or by e-mailing me through the link at my website, www.loreelough.com.

My best and God's blessings
to you and yours,
Loree

Learn to do good.
Seek justice:
help the oppressed;
defend the orphan;
plead for the widow.
— Isaiah 1:17 CEB

1

Mothers' Day Weekend at the Misty Wolf Inn
Blacksburg, Virginia

Taylor stood at the bottom of the stairs and held her breath. It only *seems* like a hundred steps, she told herself.

As she planted her foot on the first tread, Eli whispered "You really goin' up there this time?"

His hand, warm and small, fit perfectly into hers. "I'm seriously considering it," she said, nodding.

The echo of his gasp floated up and disappeared around the first bend of the long, spiral staircase. "Can I come with you?"

She followed his line of vision to the half-door leading into the turret. It had been a source of fascination for him from the moment he'd moved into the Misty Wolf Inn, nearly a year ago.

"Please, Taylor? *Please?*"

Oh, how she loved the boy who reminded

her so much of her brother! Peering into his trusting green eyes, Taylor wondered which excuse would work this time: *it's dirty and dusty up there. There are about a hundred ways you could hurt yourself. That big bare light bulb has probably burned out by now.*

But Eli beat her to the punch.

"If you let me come with you," he said, sandwiching her hand between his, "I promise to be careful and not touch anything without asking first. *Promise.*"

He'd been with her slightly more than a year now, and she could probably count on one hand the times she'd told him no. "Well," she said, pointing at his bare toes, "but only if you put on your sneakers."

He did a little jig, then fist-pumped the air. "You're the best, best, *best* aunt a boy ever had!" He ran toward his room, stopping at the halfway point. "You won't go up without me, right?"

"I'll wait right here. *Promise.*" If she didn't know better, Taylor would have said Eli's smile had inspired the "face lit up like a Christmas tree" adage. Grinning to herself, she sat on the bottom step and said a silent prayer. *Please don't let me blubber like a baby — not in front of sweet Eli.* He'd lost as many loved ones as she had, and certainly didn't need to see her fall apart. Besides, if she allowed self-pity to distract her, even for a second, he could pick up a splinter, or trip on a loose board, or topple a stack of boxes. How would she explain *that* to his grumpy uncle?

The familiar *sproing* of a doorstop broke into her thoughts, followed by thuds and thumps that inspired a grin. She could almost picture Eli, tossing shoes and boots over his shoulders as he searched for his favorite sneakers. But so what if he made a mess in his own room? The last guest had checked out last evening, and she didn't expect the next until Monday. Helping him re-tidy his closet was as good an excuse as any to give him her full, undivided attention.

He ran toward her, the soles of his shoes squeaking on the hardwood as he came to a quick stop. "See?" he said, showing her one foot, then the other. "Shoes!"

"Yep," she said, laughing, "shoes." Not the bright red high-tops she'd bought as his reward for mastering the art of tying his own shoes, but a pair of his old Velcro-closure sneakers. That he'd chosen to save time by wearing them told Taylor just how excited he was about exploring the turret's attic space.

"Well," he said, snapping on the light

switch, "are you ready?"

Ready as I'll ever be, she thought as he darted up the stairs. She'd been putting this off far too long. It was long past time to face her past — the good memories and the sad ones too.

When she caught up with Eli, she found him grunting and grimacing as he wrapped both hands around the cut-glass doorknob. "It's . . . it's stuck." Rubbing his palms together, both brows disappeared into blond bangs. "Or maybe it's locked."

Taylor hadn't been much older than Eli when her grandfather helped her hang the old skeleton key from the hook he'd hidden along the door jamb. She reached for it, then scooped Eli into her arms instead. "Quick, grab the key," she ground out. "You're heavier than you look!"

It took a second or two for him to wiggle it free, and when he did, Eli shouted "Got it!"

Taylor gave him a little squeeze before turning him loose.

Eli held it up to the light. "Never saw anything like *this* before." One eye narrowed suspiciously, he looked up at Taylor. "You sure it's a key?"

Down on one knee, she showed him how to insert it into the keyhole. "I'm sure."

After a moment of wiggling and jiggling, the lock went *clunk,* startling Eli. "Whoa!" he said, giggling as he handed Taylor the key, "bet Tootie heard that all the way over at her place!"

He grabbed the doorknob again, but this time, his hand jerked back so quickly that she couldn't help wondering if a chip in the glass had scratched him. Taylor was about to inspect his fingers when Eli said, "Is it okay if I open it, or do you want to?"

So, he'd been sincere about his promise not to touch anything without permission. Smiling, she said, "No, *you* do it."

The old brass hinges squealed as the door swung into the hallway. "It's kinda like the door on the Keebler elves' hollow tree, isn't it?"

"You know, you're absolutely right!"

Hands on his knees and shaking his head, he stooped and peered into the darkness. "We can't both fit through at the same time."

Translation: *I'm scared to go* in *first, but I want to* be *first to see what's on the other side of this strange little door.*

"I have an idea," she said, taking his hand. "I'll go in just far enough to turn on the light, and that way, we'll both see what's in there at the same time."

"Good idea!"

Side by side, they ducked through the opening. Their entry stirred a thousand dust motes that danced like microscopic ballerinas on the beam of sunlight that poured in through the front-facing window.

"Wow," Eli said, straightening. *"Wow."*

She knew exactly how he felt. As a girl, she'd spent hundreds of hours here, spinning dreams when the sun was up, wishing on the stars when moonlight painted everything — especially that gigantic old steamer trunk — a strange and eerie shade of silver.

He turned in a slow circle. "Just *look* at all this stuff!" Then he noticed the rugged wood steps that led higher still in the turret, and pointed. "What's up there?"

"Oh, just more stuff." Taylor smiled, remembering how after Nonna's stroke left her unable to sew, Grampa stacked boxes of material and spools of thread as high as his arms would allow. "*Lots* more stuff."

"Man-o-man-o-man. It'll take days to see it all!"

Yes, it probably would — if she had any desire to rouse gloomy memories.

Eli flicked a wooden whirligig, and while giggling at its comical dance, blew the dust from a red metal fire truck. "Whoa. C-o-o-ol," he said, picking it up. "Whose was it?"

"Careful, now," she warned. "There are lots of sharp edges on toys that were manufactured way back when." She held out her hand so that he could see the bright white scar in the web between her thumb and forefinger. "I got this playing with an old car that belonged to Grampa Hank's dad."

Nodding, he said, "I'll be careful." He touched the tarnished key on the side of the fire truck. "What's this thing do?"

"It makes the siren work. At least, it used to. It's an antique, and nobody has played with it in years."

He gave the key two quick cranks and grinned when the toy emitted a tinny, high-pitched wail. Down on his hands and knees, he rolled the truck back and forth. "Vroom-vroom!" he said, oblivious to the tracks its tires left in the dust.

Taylor knelt too — in front of the cedar hope chest that had lured her up here in the first place. A wedding gift from Taylor's maternal great-great-grandparents to their only daughter, it had been handed down through the generations until, on Taylor's sixteenth birthday, it became hers. For years, it stood at the foot of her bed, pestering her to look inside. Two days after hiring Isaac, she silenced the nagging by asking him to carry it to the turret.

And it had been here ever since. Would she have the courage today?

Eli put the truck back where he'd found it and went to the window. "Gosh," he said, using the heel of his hand to rub dust from the bubbly glass, "you can see all the way to the creek from up here."

"On a clear day," she said, tracing a burl in the trunk's rounded lid, "you can see even farther than that."

"Bet Uncle Reece would love this place. Wonder what he'd say if he came up here and saw all this."

Taylor harrumphed. No doubt he'd say something like, *The boy should be outside, playing in the fresh air, instead of inhaling all this grit and grime. There are probably millions of dust mites up here, along with a hundred ways he could hurt himself!*

With most people, Taylor gave people the benefit of the doubt. Why not Reece?

Maybe, she thought, because he acts more like a grumpy old codger than the thirty-something man he is.

But that wasn't fair, and she knew it. Eli might as well be Reece's only living relative after the way his parents treated him. It couldn't have been easy, finding out the way he did, that his sister hadn't named him Eli's guardian.

She remembered that day in the lawyer's office, when Reece's expression went from stunned to angry to anguished as the attorney read the paragraph in Margo's will that gave Taylor total control of the boy. The news had shocked and puzzled her, too. For one thing, she'd only known Margo since shortly before her marriage to Eliot. For another, Reece had changed his entire life to help out after Eliot was killed in Afghanistan.

Eli's excited voice pulled Taylor's attention back to the here and now. "Oh, wow," he said from his perch on the window ledge, "I can see our horses! There's Millie. And Alvin and Bert. And Elsie, too!" With each one he pointed out, Eli left a tiny fingerprint on the dusty glass. "And a whole bunch of deer. Taylor! Come see! There must be fifty of 'em!"

She loved how he called everything at the Misty Wolf "ours," from the big house itself to the land surrounding it. Taylor went to him, and hugging him from behind, said, "That *is* a big herd, isn't it! And you're right . . . we *can* see the horses from up here." It still amazed her that, almost from his first day here, he'd started referring to the Misty Wolf Inn as *home.* Even more astounding was how quickly he'd accepted the fact that his dad had been killed by a roadside bomb in Afghanistan, and a car crash had taken his mom. *Oh to have the pure, unquestioning faith of a child,* she thought, thanking God for the green-eyed blessing who stood in the circle of her arms.

"Can we go riding later?"

"Maybe . . . if there's time. It's Friday, don't forget."

"Oh, yeah. I almost forgot. An Uncle Reece Friday."

"Mmm-hmm." Uncle Reece Fridays . . . her least favorite nights of the month.

"Can I call him, see if he can come get me a little early, and maybe go riding *with* us?"

"I don't see why not. As my grandpa used to say 'It never hurts to ask.' "

One of two things would happen when they got downstairs: Eli would get busy doing little boy things and forget to make the call, or he'd get his uncle on the phone only to find out that Reece still had patients to see and wouldn't be able to leave the office early.

Turning to face her, Eli looked up into Taylor's face. "So what's in the ugly ol' trunk over there?" he asked, using his thumb as a pointer.

Taylor kissed the top of his head. "You

24

know, I honestly have no idea."

"Whose is it?"

"Mine."

"Whoa. No way. It's yours, and you don't know what's in it!"

Smiling, Taylor shrugged. " 'Fraid not."

"But . . ." His eyes widened as he looked at the trunk. "Why not? Did somebody say you weren't allowed to?"

"No."

"That you'd get in trouble for opening it?"

"No, nothing like that."

Frowning, he said, "Then . . . then why haven't you opened it!"

How could she explain to this bighearted boy — who'd lost both parents in less than a year's time — that she didn't have the guts to look at reminders of the people *she'd* lost?

"I don't have a good reason." In truth, Taylor didn't have *any* reason.

"You know that's just *weird,* don't you?"

"Yes, yes, I suppose it is."

Eli crossed both arms over his chest. "So, what do you *think* is in there?"

"Oh," she said with a sigh, "probably just a bunch of old junk. A few things that belonged to my mom and dad, and to my grandparents, maybe even *your* dad."

Eyes narrowed slightly, Eli said, "Oh. I get it. You don't want to see all that stuff 'cause you're afraid it will make you sad . . ."

"Well, I-I —"

". . . and remind you how much you miss them, right?"

She pictured Eliot's gap-toothed grin, her dad's playful wink, her mom's loving smile. "Right."

He took her hand, gave it a little squeeze. "You know what I do when I miss my mom?"

Taylor didn't know if she had the self-control to keep her tears at bay if he continued.

"I hug their pictures *re-e-eal* tight."

"*. . . because that's all I have left of them,*" Taylor finished. Stirrings of resentment swirled in her heart. She'd never forgive his mom for giving away everything that might have reminded Eli of her and his dad. *Makes it real hard to believe your death was an accident, Margo,* Taylor thought. But bitterness quickly gave way to a blush of shame as she realized what Eli was *really* telling her: *you should be thanking God that you have these things to help you remember your loved ones.*

"It'll be okay," he said, patting her hand. "I'll be right here with you. Don't worry, if you get sad, I'll give you a hug."

With that, Eli led her over to the trunk. "There's nothing in there to be scared of," he said, getting down on one knee. "There's probably nothing in there but old lady underwear!"

He giggled at his little joke as Taylor marveled at the depth of his perceptiveness. "Bummer!" he said, tugging at the big padlock. "Did your grampa lock *every*thing up?"

"Pretty much," she admitted, picturing dead bolts on the tool shed and barn, the garage, and the slanting doors leading into the basement.

"Oh, cool!" Eli said, pointing at a tarnished skeleton key. It dangled from a yard-long strand of twine that had been tied around one of the trunk's leather handles. "Must be something pretty good in there," he said, inserting it into the keyhole.

Her heartbeat doubled when the latch went *click* because now, she couldn't turn back. The sound bounced from sun-faded bureaus, threadbare chairs, framed photos, and fading portraits that stood like somber sentries against the turret's curved walls.

Eli sat back on his heels. "Well?"

Taylor might have said, *Well what?* if she could have found her voice.

27

"You want me to open it, or are you gonna do it?"

What I want, she thought, *is to go down-stairs, right now, and put Isaac to work install-ing a big lock on the door to the turret.* After which, she'd throw away the key.

Eli must have read her hesitation as permission to open the trunk because that's exactly what he did. "What's that smell?" he wanted to know.

"It's cedar, a much less stinky way to protect clothes than moth balls." Her hands shook as she removed a layer of tissue paper.

"What's that?"

"A cigar box," she said, peeling away the bulky burlap wrapper. Hands trembling, she handed it to Eli, who flipped up the lid to expose a jumble of gold chains, once-silvery earrings, bangle bracelets, rings, and a cameo broach the size of an egg.

"Oh, yuck," Eli grumbled, frowning as he handed it back. "Nothin' but *girl* stuff." Then he pointed. "Wonder what's in *there?*"

Taylor set the cigar box aside to retrieve a small wooden cedar chest. Inside, wrapped in brown paper, were dozens of scallop-edged photos, some still wearing the corner tabs that had once fastened them to the pages of an old-fashioned picture album. But sensing Eli's impatience, Taylor put the box down. She'd have plenty of time to look through the photographs after Eli left for his weekend with Reece.

In the next layer of the trunk, three elegant hats: a simple veiled pillbox, one adorned with ostrich plumes, and a straw sunbonnet trimmed in velvet. Here, a lacy-edged scarf; there, a crocheted shawl, and a single elbow-length glove that was missing one of its iridescent pearl buttons. Then, a white box filled with embroidered handkerchiefs, a package of seamed silk stockings, and finally, a wedding gown, veil, and size-five white satin shoes — all preserved to perfection in their blankets of cotton-soft tissue.

Eli exhaled a heavy sigh. "Aw, is it *all* girl stuff?"

"Sorry, kiddo," she said, mussing his bangs, "but it looks that way. But just as soon as we put everything back the way we found it, we'll open another box. And who knows," she added, tapping the tip of his upturned nose, "maybe that one will be filled with all sorts of cool *boy* stuff!"

"Want me to help?"

"No, you go ahead and play. Just be careful; some of that stuff is sharp, remember."

As he busied himself with the whirligig and the fire truck, Taylor noticed a brown cardboard box at the very bottom of the trunk; on its lid, her mother's beautifully feminine script spelled out "To Taylor."

Was it coincidence that Taylor found the box today — the Friday before Mothers' Day — her very first as a substitute mom? She didn't think so. Hands trembling and heart pounding, Taylor eased off the lid. And under a blanket of pale pink tissue paper, she saw an unfinished quilt, scraps of cloth, spools of thread, and a pencil sketch of what her mother had in mind when the project began. "Oh, my," she whispered, hugging it to her chest, "isn't it just lovely."

Eli knee-walked closer to get a better look, lips moving as he counted a dozen colorful squares cut from satin and silk, cotton and flannel. Then he picked up a small, square envelope and handed it to Taylor. "What's this?"

Taylor's fingers were shaking when she took it from him.

"Is it a note? From your *mom*?"

Nodding, she bit down hard on her lower lip. *Oh, Lord,* she prayed silently, *please don't let me cry.*

"I can read a little," Eli said, peering over her shoulder, "but Mrs. Cunningham hasn't taught us cursive yet."

Despite her astonishment at finding the

quilt, Taylor picked up on Eli's not-so-subtle hint. She slid the ivory notepaper from its matching envelope and cleared her throat.

"To sweet Taylor, my precious little gift from God," she read, "I pray this will keep you warm, not only on this, your 7th birthday, but every day of your life. I will also pray that it will always remind you how very much you are loved and treasured, for you are my heart, dear one!"

And it was signed *Your loving mother.*

For what seemed a full five minutes, Eli sat quietly, nodding. And then he said, "I get it. Your mom died before she could finish your birthday present, didn't she?"

The sheen of tears in his big green eyes told Taylor that he really *did* get it. Unable to speak past the sob aching in her throat, she drew him into a hug.

"Family," he said into her shoulder, "is the most important thing in the whole wide world."

"Yes," she whispered. "Yes, it sure is!"

"I'm really glad," he said, looking into her face, "that your mom made you something to remember her by." He looked back at the unfinished quilt. "Well, at least she tried to, anyway." He met her eyes to add "You're glad about that, right?"

Yes, of course she was, but not so glad

that she hadn't heard the note of regret in Eli's sweet voice: *his* mom hadn't left anything for him to remember her by and (thanks to Margo's closet-cleaning frenzy) neither had Eliot.

Eli leaned into the trunk, his voice echoing as he said, "Hey, look at this!" Sitting back on his heels, he held up his find. "It's a pearl." He held it between thumb and forefinger to inspect it. "Do you think it's real?"

"No," she said as he handed it to her, "probably not." She showed him the glove with the missing button. "I think it belongs here."

His tiny finger ruffled the threads, still dangling from the glove's wrist. "You gonna sew it back on?"

"Probably not," she said again, "since the glove doesn't have a mate. But I'll save the button. Who knows where it might end up?" Snickering, she tousled his hair. "Maybe on your soccer uniform!"

Eyes wide, he cringed. "No way! Eww! *Yuck!*"

Taylor pulled him close and said, "You know I'm only teasing, right?"

"Yeah. 'Course I do." But his smile faded as he glanced at the unfinished quilt. He didn't have to voice his wish aloud for Taylor to know what it was: *wish my mom and dad left me stuff like this to remember them by.*

As she searched her heart and mind for *just* the right words to comfort and reassure him, a shard of sunlight glinted from the button and exploded in a dazzling rainbow arc that radiated blue and green, pink and purple. It lasted an eye blink, a heartbeat, a mere spark in time before disappearing like the horizon's illusive green flash . . .

. . . exactly long enough for an idea to begin taking shape in her mind.

2

Few things irked Reece more than knowing he'd lost control of a situation, and he'd felt anything *but* in charge of the meeting with his realtor. It wasn't Wesley's fault that the market was in such miserable shape, or that Reece would take a financial beating no matter which house he put on the market. So why had he stomped from the office like the proverbial bull in a china shop?

It seemed like he'd been in this foul mood for more than a year, starting on that blustery day last April when his sister's lawyer hit him with the awful news: *Taylor Bradley* would get custody of Eli! Taylor, whose Misty Wolf Inn attracted musicians and artists and all sorts of weirdos and nut jobs. Taylor, who wore too much mascara and jangly jewelry and flowing skirts. Taylor, whose idiot brother promised to remain stateside but went back on his word and got himself killed four days after rejoining his unit in Afghanistan . . . making Margo a widow and leaving little Eli fatherless.

To be fair, it wasn't Taylor's fault that every time he saw her, he was reminded of Eliot. She'd looked as shocked as he'd felt when Moses Adams read those life-altering words, dictated by Margo herself. Reece had studied enough psychology while earning his MD to recognize his ire for what it was: misplaced hostility. But just because Taylor hadn't started the legal ball rolling didn't make it any easier to admit that Eli seemed to prefer her company to his.

Better watch it, Montgomery, he warned, *or you'll end up looking and sounding as grumpy as old Amos himself.*

He tried reflecting on more positive things, like the fact that, in less than half an hour, Eli would be belted into his booster seat in the back, inundating him with a thousand and one questions: What holds the clouds in the sky? Why do some cars make so much noise? Who decides the speed limit? How do policemen become policemen? Thinking about that alone was enough to make him relax enough to appreciate that the scenery — from Cassell Coliseum to the Blue Ridge Mountains and the Appalachians — made the intolerable *reason* for the trip a little more tolerable.

But really he didn't have any more business complaining about the drive than he had for grumbling about the schedule. It had been *Taylor's* idea to alternate holidays and weekends with Eli.

Reece checked his side mirror, then passed an eighteen-wheeler, remembering as he put it behind him how awkward they'd all felt in the moments following Moses' announcement that Margo picked Taylor for Eli's legal guardian. A flurry of emotions had flashed across her pretty face, from shock and disbelief to joy and, finally, compassion as she realized what *he* must be feeling, hearing the news. She'd blinked back big silvery tears, and clearing her throat, said, "Surely there's some mistake, Mr. Adams." And even after Moses pointed at the clause in Margo's will and insisted it was all there in black and white, she refused to accept it as fact. "But . . . but why *me,* when Dr. Montgomery is, well, he's a *doctor.* A *pediatrician* no less! He gave up so much to help Margo after Eliot died. I just can't believe she'd —"

Moses silenced her with a raised hand and made it clear that it was his job to draw up the papers, not second-guess his clients' decisions.

But that didn't satisfy her either. Taylor

leaned into the space between her chair and his. Leaned so close, in fact, that Reece had inhaled a whiff of her flowery shampoo. "If we can talk him into drawing up the paperwork," she'd whispered, "would you be okay with spending every other weekend with Eli?"

She'd said more, but to this day, he couldn't remember *what,* specifically, because he'd been too busy trying to figure out why she'd suggest such a thing. He didn't know how long he might have sat there, staring like a gap-mouthed dunderhead, if she hadn't added, "I'm happy to pay for it if Mr. Adams charges for the addendum. Anything for Eli."

His grip tightened on the steering wheel. Anything for Eli, indeed.

Reece had cosigned the loan for Eliot and Margo's sprawling rancher . . . *for Eli.* Now, with both of them gone, he'd kept up the payments, thinking to sell the place at some point, an investment in Eli's future. He'd hold onto the hideous mass of wood and glass indefinitely . . . if he thought for a minute Eli might want it someday.

But the boy hadn't made a single reference to the house where he'd spent the first three years of his life. In fact, the casual observer would find it hard to believe he hadn't been born in Taylor's B&B, because *that's* the place Eli called home.

And that wasn't Taylor's fault either.

"Thanks for nothin', sis," he muttered as a car no bigger than a breath mint sped by on his left. Any minute now, the big elaborate sign at the end of Taylor's drive would appear alongside the road. Last thing he wanted was to show up with a head of steam, the way he had two Sundays ago, when it dawned on him that Margo's death *hadn't* been an accident. Despite the depression that kept her in a drug-induced fog, she'd managed to map everything out, right down to making a list of the stuff Eli was allergic to. He'd been so mad at himself for taking so long to figure it out that when he'd arrived at the B&B red-faced, Taylor suggested he crank up the A/C for the drive home.

As if on cue, the bright white fences surrounding her corral came into view. She didn't keep many horses — four, maybe five — and he gave credit where credit was due. Just enough to entertain her equine-loving guests, he thought, but not so many that their care and vet bills would eat up precious time and money.

Was it his imagination or was the smallest one looking at him now?

Reece slowed his Mustang. Sure enough, the dapple gray ran alongside the fence, keeping pace with his sedate black sedan, purchased solely because there wasn't space in his two-seater Alfa Romeo for Eli's booster seat. The dashboard clock said 4:31. He had time to stop, give the animal a pat on the nose. It whinnied as he pressed harder on the gas pedal. "Maybe next time," he said, looking into the rearview mirror. "And maybe not."

The terrifying episode from his childhood still haunted his dreams — not as often as it once had — but more than enough to make him squeeze the steering wheel even tighter. Before it happened, his grandfather used to call him Saddle Pants, because Reece loved to ride and did it every chance he got. If he'd taken Pop's advice and got right back into the saddle, he might own a horse or two of his own.

Taylor's white mailbox appeared, luring him back to the here and now. Beside it, the big welcoming sign:

Reece knew that Taylor had designed and built it because Eli had told him so — nearly every time he steered the car down the winding gravel path that ribboned from the road to the horseshoe drive at her front porch. He'd also boasted about how Taylor had let him paint the framelike border around the majestic wolf. Reece had to hand it to her because it must have taken a world of patience to guide those energetic little fingers. . . .

He'd seen a few of her sketches and watercolors in the foyer and had to admit Taylor was quite the artist. And based on the soups and stews, breads and desserts she routinely packed up for him to take home, Reece had good reason to say that her talents with pencils and paintbrushes paled by comparison to her culinary skills.

Today, unless his nose was mistaken, she'd

baked chocolate chip cookies, and the aroma started his mouth watering even before he rang the bell. "Come on in," she called. "I'm in the kitchen."

A flash of metal caught his eye and he slowed his steps, immediately recognizing it as the screw-mechanism of an embroidery hoop, protruding from one of the compartments of a white wicker sewing basket. In nearly every memory of his grandmother, she held a hoop much like this one as she stitched colorful birds and butterflies onto handkerchiefs, tablecloths, and pillowcases. She had a sewing basket like this one, too. If he opened the lids and drawers, would he find thread, scissors, curved needles, and other dangerous tools among the multicolored scraps of cloth?

Whether it belonged to one of Taylor's guests or the innkeeper, herself, he aimed to find out what careless fool had left it out in the open, well within reach of a bright, curious child like Eli. Reece followed the thick burgundy runner, wondering how to broach the subject in a nonconfrontational way.

"Sorry I'm early," he said, pushing through the cafe doors. "Traffic's not usually this light on a Friday evening."

After a quick glance at the schoolhouse

clock above the sink, Taylor waved his apology away. "Oh, don't give it another thought." She went back to dropping cookie dough onto parchment-lined trays. "But your nephew and his best buddy, Randy, aren't here, I'm afraid. Isaac invited Tootie on a picnic, and the boys sort of horned in." She shrugged. "They were supposed to be back half an hour ago, but when that foursome gets together, they lose all track of time." It pleased Reece to hear that Randy could still participate in normal little-boy things.

He remembered the day, just over a year ago, when he'd taken Eli to the office to spend the day with his secretary, Maureen, and his nurse, Gina. The mother-daughter team ran the place with military efficiency and won the heart of his little nephew when he was still in diapers. That day, while they showed Eli how the baby scales worked, Reece broke the news to Randy's recently widowed mom that test results and consults with pulmonary and orthopedic specialists had confirmed his worst suspicions: her only child had Duchenne's Dystrophy. At three years of age, Randy had no idea what challenges lay ahead, but Mrs. Clayton understood. Eli — God love him — sensing the gravity of the situation, hopped up onto the reception counter and belted out his off-key rendition of *Jesus Loves the Little Children.* By the time he sang the last verse, everyone was in stitches, and the boys had been pals ever since.

Reece hoped Randy had worn his back and leg braces. He felt like an ogre, prescribing the awful things, but like it or not, they were as important as the physical therapy and muscle relaxants he'd prescribed. Besides, if —

"You might as well take a load off while you wait." Taylor then pulled out the nearest of eight ladder-back chairs surrounding the big rectangular table.

And so he sat.

A good time to bring up the careless placement of the sewing basket?

Why did he feel at a loss for words? Was it because before today, Taylor always had Eli ready and waiting when he arrived, eliminating the need for small talk? Or the fact that her relaxed smile told him *she* didn't feel the least bit awkward?

She put her back to him and removed two cookie sheets from the oven, and he remembered how many times Margo had said that if Taylor had been a foot taller and seventy-five pounds heavier, people might mistake her and Eliot for twins. Yeah, they both had big gray eyes and white-blond hair, but in his opinion, the similarities began and ended right there.

On the night Margo introduced them, Taylor sandwiched his hand between hers and said, "It's a pleasure to meet you, finally!" He'd been engaged to Dixie at the time and felt an instant stab of guilt when the genuine warmth in her eyes and the soft-spoken rhythm of her words set his pulse to racing. So he'd snapped back his hand and muttered a gruff, "Right," and did his best to focus on her flaws: she hugged *every*one; laughed at jokes that weren't funny; disposed of other people's empty plates and refilled cups without being asked to. When that proved pointless, he repeated the old "If someone seems too good to be true, they *are*" rule.

It's what he told himself at the wedding reception, in the waiting room on the night Eli was born, at every family gathering since . . . and ran headlong into the same frustrating lack of success. Now, as she puttered around her kitchen looking more appealing than she had a right to in her pink-and-white checked apron, he searched his brain for something, *any*thing to criticize, and came up —

"Can I pour you some iced tea while you wait?"

Hopefully, fussing with the cookies had kept her too preoccupied to notice that he'd been gawking like a moony-eyed schoolboy.

"Or maybe you'd rather have lemonade . . ."

"Is it fresh-squeezed?" What difference does *that* make! he thought, groaning inwardly.

"But, of course."

Reece almost chuckled at the way she said it . . . as if in her mind, that was the *only* kind. He might have pointed out that he'd learned the hard way that the powdered stuff couldn't compare with fresh-squeezed . . . if she hadn't chosen that moment to start humming a little tune while she filled a glass with ice and lemonade.

He didn't know what to make of the at-ease way she behaved around him, because he sure as shootin' hadn't done anything to earn it. Unless mind reading was another of her many talents, she couldn't know that he'd spent this past year dumping pent-up resentments toward Eliot onto Taylor, mostly because of their spooky physical resemblance. The admission rattled him more than he cared to admit.

"Goodness," she said as he pulled out a

chair, "is the lemonade that sour?"

"Sour? No, it's great. Perfect." And to prove it, he drank every last drop, then smiled. Smiled way too big and way too long, if that puzzled look on her pretty face was any indicator. He held up the tumbler, as if offering a toast. "You'll have to give me the recipe. So I can make it for Eli. When he's at my place." He smacked his lips. "Because it's really good."

Taylor picked up his cue for a refill, and when she handed the glass back, their fingers touched for a nanosecond . . . exactly long enough to send his heart into overdrive. *Better get a grip, pal. . . .*

"It's pretty easy-peasy," she said with a wink. "Four ripe lemons. Half cup of sugar. Pitcher of water. The trick is . . . you have to roll the lemons really well before you cut and squeeze them."

Reece nodded. "Aha." If he sounded distracted, well, was it his fault she put her whole body into every word she spoke?

And then he thought of something that would help him hold her feet to the fire. "About that sewing basket in your front hall . . ."

"Oh, my goodness," she said. "I'm so glad you reminded me! I had every good intention of putting it upstairs in my room, so I can start on a special project for Eli while he's away for the weekend. He doesn't usually get into things like that, like some kids do, but why take chances, y'know?"

While he was thinking, *Yeah, yeah, right . . . I know,* Taylor dashed out of the room. "Be right back," she said, "just as soon as I put it out of his reach."

While she was gone, he got up, sauntered over to the stove and lifted the lid of the big silvery kettle he'd been eyeballing almost from the moment he walked into the room.

"It's spaghetti sauce," she said, stepping up to the sink to wash her hands. "It's a special request from a special guest who's checking in tonight."

He replaced the pot lid, thinking, special guest — singular; just exactly *how* special? Not that it was any of his business. Then again, if the guest was some guy who held a special place in her heart . . . Eli spent most of his time in this house with Taylor. Didn't that *make* it his business?

"Eli calls it 'Tay-getti,' " she said, drying her hands, "because I make the sauce from scratch." She grabbed a teaspoon from the drawer beside the stove. After filling it with thick, rich sauce, she handed it to Reece.

The aroma alone had the power to make a grown man swoon. "Delicious," he admitted, wishing she'd chosen a tablespoon, instead.

"Then I'll pack some up for you to take home. I'm sure after dealing with sick kids all week, the last thing you feel like doing is cooking."

"I don't mind cooking. In fact, I *like* doing things for Eli." What was it about her that made him feel so . . . so *defensive*? Because she was just about perfect? Or because she made perfect look so easy? He bought time to mull it over by taking a gulp of the lemonade. "This really is some delicious stuff." And then he frowned. First defensive, then effusive. He really *did* need to get a grip!

Reece took another swig and tried again. "I, um, I thought maybe I'd take Eli to the diner on the way home. He loves their Mile-High Meatloaf. And afterward, we'll catch that singing rodents movie."

"Rats!"

He almost said, *No, not rats.* Good thing he'd kept his big mouth shut, because she followed it up with "If only I had known. I took him to see that one last Saturday."

A couple of Reece's pals were every-other-weekend dads, and often complained about how tough it was, trying to top what their exes did for and with the kids. Shouldn't their primary concern be that the kids were loved and properly cared for? The guys couldn't buy their kids' love, so why even try? Didn't they realize how small-minded and petty they sounded, comparing apples to oranges that way?

Well, he didn't feel that way right now. *Now* he understood how bad it felt to be one-upped, especially when he'd put so much effort into making his weekends with Eli fun. And memorable. So that maybe, just once in a while, the kid would call *his* house "home."

Taylor chose that moment to aim a dainty finger at the ceiling, almost making him forget his indignation.

Almost.

"While they were running the previews, Eli got *all* excited about seeing that dolphin movie. Maybe you could take him to see that one instead. Have you seen the commercials?"

"Can't say that I have." He could spout his I'm-a-doctor viewpoint on too much TV-watching. Maybe then *she'd* be on the defensive for a change.

But Taylor was busy filling plastic containers with sauce-drenched noodles, extra sauce, and home-baked bread, chattering as she pressed their lids into place. Still chattering as she stacked them into a small Styrofoam cooler: now he'd have one less meal to prepare. Which meant he could spend more time with Eli. Just plop the stuff onto plates — because the experts said "nuked plastic" might contain carcinogens — and pop 'em into the microwave. No need to worry about returning the tubs because she had mountains of them stacked up in the pantry.

So. It seemed Miss Perfect had thought of everything. Again. Except the possibility that he might have other plans, like making pizza for Eli on Saturday and grilling burgers on Sunday.

She was loading a shoebox-sized tin with chocolate chip cookies when Reece wondered why he even bothered to compare himself to her. Like everything else she tackled, Taylor had turned taking care of others into an art form. No way a ham-fisted bachelor whose cooking aptitude could be described with two words — frozen and prepackaged — was supposed to compete with that.

He glanced at his watch. If he and Eli didn't get out of here soon, there wouldn't be time for supper at the diner before the movie. Well, there was always tomorrow. And it wasn't like they'd starve, thanks to all the food she'd tucked into that cooler. "So how many horses do you have?"

"Just four. Although sometimes," she said, laughing, "I think it's three too many."

"Yeah. I imagine they're a lot of work."

"Some days are easier than others, but I've worked out a pretty good system. As long as I stick to the schedule, things go much more smoothly."

Reece listened intently as she ran down the daily, weekly, and monthly chores lists. The gal had her flaws, but laziness sure wasn't one of them.

"But I can't take credit for how pretty the horses look. Isaac takes care of trimming their manes and tails."

She put a couple of still-warm cookies onto a dessert plate, and sat it on the table near his elbow. "Funny you should mention the horses today."

"Oh? Why?" he said around a bite.

Arms crossed over her ruffly apron, she said, "Because just this morning, Eli asked if he could call you, see if you wanted to get here a little early, go riding with us."

"Why didn't he?"

"He tried. Said he kept getting a 'buzzy' signal." She punctuated it with another giggle.

"Bummer. I would have loved that." He

took a swig of lemonade to hide the fib. "But it was a crazy day."

"Patients all afternoon, huh?"

"Yeah, 'fraid so."

One well-arched brow rose on her forehead, and he knew just as sure as he was sitting there that she sensed the "but" in his statement.

She'd never struck him as the judgmental type; what could it hurt to admit the truth? "But . . ." Reece shrugged. "I'm afraid of horses anyway, so . . ."

"Oh, you wouldn't believe how many people are! Until they learn a few simple tricks, that is." She tilted her head to add "If you want to learn, I'm happy to teach you."

He had to hand it to her. Not only had she glossed right over his flat-out admission of fear, she'd offered a no-pressure solution. "It's something to think about, for sure."

"That nephew of ours *loves* to ride." She went back to stacking cookies in a big plastic tub. "So if you learned, you could ride together. Any time. For as long as you please."

A no-pressure suggestion, followed by a no-obligation invitation. And all without the customary "If you *don't* do it, you're an ungrateful lout" guilt trip attached.

Reece cleared his throat. "Ah, does Tootie have a cell phone?"

She prefaced her answer with a tiny snicker, which told him she'd picked up on his "Can we change the subject, fast?" tack.

"Oh, she's had one for years. Trouble is, half the time, she forgets to take it with her. And the other half," she said on a sigh, "she forgets to turn it on." Another laugh. "And the rest of the time? She forgets to charge it!"

He'd only met Taylor's next-door neighbor a few times, and even then, only in passing. Frankly, Reece didn't understand why Tootie and Taylor were so close. Except for their gender — and the connection to Taylor's handyman — the women didn't have a thing in common. "What about Isaac? Does he have a cell? I don't mean to rush anybody, but I had plans to —"

"Uncle Reece!" Eli bellowed, hurtling himself across the room and into Reece's arms.

Instantly, negative thoughts and dark memories of Margo and Eliot melted away. "Hey, li'l buddy, how was your picnic?"

"Aw, man . . . it was *great*! Isaac taught me an' Randy how to bait a fishhook. And then I caught a trout. And Randy caught a Muskie." His brow furrowed slightly. "Only, we can't cook 'em, though, on account-a Tootie made us throw 'em back." He rolled his eyes, then shrugged. "But that's okay, 'cause she taught us how to whistle real loud. Well, not *us,* 'cause Randy's still workin' on it, but *I* learned. Listen. . . ."

The boy made an O of his thumb and forefinger and stuck it between his upper and lower teeth, and cut loose with an ear-piercing blast.

Laughing, Reece winced. "Whoa, I think maybe you just broke the sound barrier!"

"You think if I do that at an Orioles game some time, the team will look up, and maybe throw me a foul ball?"

"I don't see why not." Reece hadn't told Eli yet about his main birthday present: tickets to every one of the Birds' home games. He'd already reserved a suite at the Sheraton, a short walk from Camden Yards, and called in a favor or two that would put them in the locker room a time or two. He felt fairly certain that Taylor would swap weekends, as she'd been more than accommodating when patient emergencies forced him to reschedule; the least he could do was run it by her before getting Eli all ramped up about things.

He'd do it now . . . if she and Tootie didn't have their heads together, whispering and snickering. He heard "Isaac" and "date," something about wildflowers and sneezing, and stifled an amused groan. "Ready to hit the road, kiddo?"

Eli looked at Taylor. "Am I ready to hit the road?"

"Your bag is in the front hall, right next to the door, same as always."

Grinning, he pointed at the white Styrofoam cooler on the floor near the restaurant-size fridge. "Is that for me and Uncle Reece, too?"

Arms folded across her chest, she grinned. "Sure is."

"I hope there's Tay-getti in it."

She winked. "And meatballs, too."

He rubbed his palms together. "Just wait 'til you taste 'em, Uncle Reece. You'll think you're in heaven!"

Reece remembered the sauce taste-test and unconsciously licked his lips. "I believe you," he said, even though it had been a long, long time since he'd believed in *heaven.* Too many of his contemporaries felt that allowing children to believe in Santa, the Easter Bunny, and the Tooth Fairy was unhealthy, but Reece didn't agree. He'd only been slightly older than Eli when a fifth grader on the school bus decided — a week before Christmas — to make sure the younger passengers got an earful of The Truth According to Mike Baggett. In a few months, Reece would turn 37, yet memory of that day *still* had the power to make him frown. If Eli — who, at four, had already faced more of life's harsh realities than most adults — drew some comfort from believing there's a loving God up in heaven, no way would Reece take it away from him.

Besides, anybody could see how happy and well-adjusted he was, and Reece knew that Taylor was largely responsible for that. A decent man would thank her, but when it came to matters involving Taylor Bradley, Reece felt anything *but* decent.

Take now, for example, as ire built inside him, watching Taylor lean against the sink, one sneakered foot crossed over the other and frowning at the screen of her iPhone. If he lived to be a hundred, Reece would never figure out why some people couldn't seem to get ten feet from the devices without going into detox. If he didn't make tracks, he might just be tempted to say so, out loud.

"Ready, Eli?"

"Yup! Are we goin' to the diner, like you said on the phone the other day?"

"Yup."

"And then to the movies?"

He opened his mouth to say, *You bet we*

are! when Taylor looked up from her phone.

"You're in luck, boys!" She tapped the phone's screen. "I just checked, and that movie you wanted to see is playing tonight. Seven-fifteen. So there's time for Mile-High Meatloaf before the show starts."

"You mean the movie about the dolphin?"

She put her phone on the counter and clapped her hands. "One and the same!"

"Way cool!" Eli said.

Then he grabbed Reece's hand. He grabbed Taylor's, too, and as Eli walked between them into the foyer, Reece felt like a heel for lumping her in with every other cell phone addict out there.

Crouching, she held Eli's face in her hands. "Have a great time," she said, kissing his forehead, "and I'll see you on Sunday."

She didn't remind Eli to brush his teeth and take his vitamins. Didn't tell him to get to bed on time or zip his jacket if he went outside, the way his buddies claimed their exes did. Taylor's behavior wasn't anything new; he'd witnessed this cheery demeanor every other Friday. Her relaxed behavior and positive words told Eli that not only was he in good hands with his uncle, but that *she* would be fine while he was gone. It told Reece something, too: if his buddies had exes like Taylor, they probably wouldn't

57

be exes.

He realized that Eli had been watching him and Taylor. Left brow up and right eye narrowed, the better word was *scrutinizing.* Grinning, Reece thought, oh, to know what was going on in that remarkable little brain. He didn't have to wonder long, because Eli chose that moment to slap a palm over his eyes. "Oh, good grief. If you're gonna kiss her, just get it over with, will ya please?"

Taylor's rasping gasp echoed loud in the big foyer. She looked sweeter and prettier — if that was possible — blushing like a schoolgirl as one hand shaded her eyes. Reece felt obliged to get her off the hook. Putting both hands on Eli's shoulders, he turned him toward the front door. "Grab your backpack, little nut, and let's get a move on." But even as he said it, Reece knew that his words got *him* off the hook, too, because for a weird minute there, the kid's suggestion sounded mighty tempting.

Without skipping a beat, Eli asked permission to bring his ninja soldiers. "I know right where they are," he said, looking up at Reece. "It won't take me long to get them. And they're little, so they'll fit in my bag, no problem."

Reece looked to Taylor for guidance on

that one because she'd bought the toy soldiers.

"Of course you can bring them, if —"

Eli was halfway up the stairs before she finished with "if it's all right with your uncle." Then she laughed, making Reece wonder why he'd never noticed before how much *music* there was in every sound that passed her lovely lips.

"I hope he doesn't bring them *all*," she said, "because he has dozens of those crazy things."

Reece pictured the overflowing toy box in his family room, and the one just like it up in Eli's room. "And dinosaurs."

She nodded. "And Hot Wheels."

"Right, they're everywhere." He chuckled. "Like crayons."

"Oh, no kidding! I mean, seriously, does Crayola intend to replicate every color in the entire world?"

"Sure seems that way, doesn't it? And if they do, no doubt Eli will want every shade."

Small talk. Usually, he did his best to avoid it. Today? Reece didn't know what to make of the fact that he was actually *enjoying* it.

Two ninjas tumbled down the stairs, and right behind them, a fat red crayon that stopped rolling when it bumped into the baseboard, right where the sewing basket had sat, earlier. He remembered thinking that it looked a lot like the one his grandmother used to keep in her spare bedroom, right down to the little wooden balls that served as feet.

"Looks like our boy is conducting a search-and-rescue mission up there," Taylor said, rescuing the toys.

Our boy. It surprised him a little, but Reece liked the sound of that. "You'd think there was a herd of elephants up there instead of one small boy," he said with a glance at the ceiling.

"Makes you wonder about the guy who coined the phrase 'pitter-patter of little feet.' "

He laughed. "Yeah. If he'd ever met a real live kid, he'd know it's more like drumbeats."

"Or the thunder of horses' hooves."

They were laughing when Eli raced down the stairs and stood between them, clutching half a dozen ninjas and a handful of crayons to his chest. "What's so funny?" he asked, looking from Reece to Taylor and back again.

"Well, *first* of all," Taylor began, touching a fingertip to Eli's nose, "how many times have I asked you not to run in the house?"

Shoulders slumped, he exhaled a heavy sigh. "About a hundred thousand million."

Squatting, Reece said, "A hundred thousand million, eh? That's a lot of times." Winking, he gently chucked the boy's chin. "So how 'bout if we quit running indoors, then, 'cause it'd be a shame for that number to reach a hundred thousand million *and one.*"

Grinning, Eli said okay and stuffed the toys into his backpack. When he finished, he slung the bag over one shoulder. "So where's your sewing kit?"

"Upstairs, where it belongs," she said, blushing and looking a bit like a kid, caught with her hand in the proverbial cookie jar.

"You gonna hem my new jeans while I'm gone?"

"Maybe . . ."

A long-suffering groan escaped Eli's lungs. *"Now what?"*

Taylor hugged him again, longer and tighter this time. "Well, I'm sure your uncle has a mountain of toys for you over at his place. Those crayons will probably only get broken in that overstuffed bag of yours. Or lost on the floor of his car, where they'll melt in the hot sun and mess up his mats."

"Good point." He found as many as he could and dropped them into the cup Taylor made of her upturned palms. "See you Sunday," he said, popping a kiss to her cheek. "Don't poke yourself with a needle or anything, 'k?"

She followed them onto the porch and promised to be careful.

And something told Reece that he'd see her lopsided grin and that goofy crayon-fisted good-bye wave in his dreams.

3

"Friday night blues?"

Squinting, Taylor threaded the needle. Maybe feigned concentration would convince her friend and neighbor that she *didn't* miss Eli like crazy. "I think you're confused. Wasn't that movie title *Friday Night Lights*?"

Tootie helped herself to a chocolate chip cookie. "Neatly sidestepped, girlfriend. But you know what they say: you can fool some of the people some of the time, but you can *never* fool an old friend."

Taylor smiled, but her heart wasn't in it. "I wonder what Mr. Lincoln would say about the way you just tweaked his quote."

"Hmpf," Tootie said, pushing back from the table. She poured herself a cup of tea, then fixed one for Taylor. On her way back to her chair, she peeked over Taylor's shoulder. "Wow. That's some quilt. Making it for the church raffle?"

"No, my mother started it as a birthday

present for me. I found it in an old trunk this morning." Tootie knew the story only too well; hopefully, she'd let the "old trunk" line pass. But just in case, Taylor quickly added "I thought maybe I'd finish it for Eli. But not a word about it to him, you hear, because it's a secret."

"Birthday present, huh?" She grabbed two packets of sweetener from the bowl in the center of the table.

The month of May was more than half over already, and he'd turn five on the Fourth of July. "No, I don't see how I could possibly get it finished by then."

Nodding, Tootie dumped the sweetener into her mug. "Interesting pattern," she said, leaning forward, "but you know, I don't think I've ever seen anything quite like it." Her spoon clinked a dozen times as she stirred her tea. "What's it called?"

Taylor had made every quilt in the guest rooms, but none would have won county fair blue ribbons, the way Tootie's had. "I'm sort of making it up as I go along." She shrugged. "Got the idea in the attic this morning. I thought maybe I'd call it a mem—"

"Whoa. You? In the *attic*?"

Shortly after moving into the place she'd inherited from her grandparents, Taylor had given Tootie permission to snoop around in the turret, alone. Though she hadn't pressed it when Taylor flatly refused to go up there, Tootie had looked exactly as she did now: brown eyes wide with stunned disbelief.

"You wouldn't kid a kidder, would you?"

"Eli sorta talked me into it."

"Well, God bless all the li'l chil'ren."

Taylor chose to ignore Tootie's sarcasm. It wasn't her fault, after all, that Taylor couldn't explain her aversion to the place and everything in it. "While he hunted for lost treasure, I finally opened the hope chest —"

Tootie propped both elbows on the table. "Do tell."

"— and I found a box, hidden under a bunch of old hats and stuff." She hugged the quilt to her chest. The faint scent of her mother's favorite perfume, wafted into her nostrils. She could almost picture the classic Chanel No. 5 vial, reflected in the mirrored tray that sat on her long, mahogany dresser.

She told Tootie about the note, and how Eli got all choked up and teary-eyed when he admitted how lucky she was to have something to remember her mother by. And then, without any warning whatever, tears welled in *her* eyes.

Thankfully, Tootie took it as a hint to change the subject. "Think I'll start calling you the Artful Dodger. Very clever, young lady, trying to get me off track with quilt talk." She tapped her temple. "Good thing I'm not as addle-brained as I look!" Her merry laughter bounced from every surface in the kitchen. "There's no shame in admitting that you miss Eli. Heck, even *I* miss him when he's with Dr. Limpy."

Taylor only shook her head.

"What."

"I won't even comment on your crack about Reece's limp, because I'm sure it was only a slip of the tongue. But I *am* wondering what Charles Dickens would think about how you've misunderstood one of his most famous characters, that's what."

Tootie's brow furrowed. "Charles Dickens? What's he got to do with the price of tea and cookies?"

"He created Jack, *the* Artful Dodger, remember?"

Laughing, she took another cookie. "Oh. Right." She giggled. "Okay, so maybe you've never picked a pocket, but you're still a shoe-in for the 'evading issues' title." Using her cookie as a pointer, Tootie added, "And I'll bet even Dr. Haughty would admit that he misses the boy when he's with us . . . if we could get him to step down from his pedestal long enough to pose the question."

"Much as I admire that thesauruslike brain of yours, I really wish you'd stop calling him names."

"Why? It's all true. He *is* haughty, and you know it far better — and for a whole lot longer — than I do!"

"Well . . . maybe that was true in the beginning. But he's coming around. Why, most days, Reece is downright warm and friendly, and —"

"Pishposh."

Taylor continued sewing as if the interruption hadn't happened. This patch — a rectangle cut from Margo's white-satin wedding gown — demanded extra care to avoid snags. "Besides, what if one day you forget what a sweet and caring person you are, and refer to Reece as Dr. Haughty — or any one of a dozen other colorful adjectives I won't name — in front of Eli? How would I explain that!"

"Sarcasm doesn't become you," Tootie said, winking. "But seriously, girl, why should *you* have to explain it? If I ever do something that thoughtless in front of the li'l squirt, *I'll* be the one to make things right." She picked up a square of blue plaid flannel. "Even though it wouldn't change the fact that Dr. Reece Montgomery is a self-important, stuck-up, stubborn know-it-all."

"Gosh. Why don't you tell me how you *really* feel? Keeping things all bottled up inside isn't healthy, you know."

"Pishposh," she repeated.

"Anyway, you wouldn't talk about Reece that way if you knew him better." The image of him, looking anything *but* overconfident as he'd sat right where Tootie was now, made her heart do a little flip.

Tootie returned the flannel to its stack and plucked a napkin from the wrought iron holder. "So how'd he get that limp of his, Miss Knows Him Well?"

"I wondered the same thing, at first," Taylor admitted, "but a person doesn't just blurt out a question like that." She double-stitched the corner of the white satin square, then made the turn to begin a second side. "The right opening never presented itself. I figured sooner or later, the subject would come up, but it didn't."

"And you're not the least bit curious?"

"I wouldn't say *that*. . . ."

Harrumphing, Tootie removed her eyeglasses. "He probably broke his toe, kicking a three-legged dog."

"Good grief, Tootie! You talk as if he's the

troll in that billy goat fable!"

"I know what I see and hear. And if I do say so myself, I'm a pretty good judge of character, too." She huffed onto one of the lenses, polished it with the napkin. "I remember only too well what that . . . that *man* put you through after Eliot was killed." She held her glasses up to the light, then put them back on. "And I don't know *how* you can forgive him for those cold-hearted things he said to you after Margo's burial."

For years, just thinking about his scathing glare and heated words made her shy away from him at family get-togethers. "I'm sure he doesn't intend to sound so . . ." Taylor searched her mind for the right word.

". . . like a cold, callus, heartless *mule*?"

"Tootie, really. Give the guy a break, if not for me, then for Eli."

The woman picked up one of the circles Taylor had cut from Eliot's high school football uniform. Snorting, she inspected it. "What position did Eliot play?"

"Fullback."

"Sorry about the name-calling. I'll keep my opinions about the good doctor to myself from now on."

You've been doing it for years; I know that won't be easy!

"I'm not the one who has to put up with

69

him every other week."

Well, that's true enough!

"I suppose I owe it to you to at least try."

"Do or do not," she quoted Yoda, "there *is* no try."

On the heels of a frustrated sigh, Tootie said, "You know what I wish?"

No, but I'm sure you're about to tell me.

"I wish that once, just *once,* I could catch you on a day when your halo is in the shop."

"When my . . ." Taylor laughed. "What does *that* mean!"

"How long have we been friends, Taylor?"

"Leave it to you to answer a question with a question," she teased.

"Yeah, yeah, I know, it's an Irish thing. Just humor me, will ya?"

Taylor did a quick mental tally of the years. "Since you carried that gorgeous rosebush all the way over here to welcome me to the neighborhood. Just a little over six years ago, if my math isn't off."

"It isn't. You moved here on my birthday, April 13th. It fell on Friday that year, remember?"

"As a matter of fact, I do. . . ." And she remembered thinking that for a never-miss-a-service Christian, Tootie sure was big on superstitions.

"Meeting you changed my notion that

Friday the 13th was an unlucky day."

"It was a pretty lucky day for me, too." Because Tootie had pretty much been a fixture around the inn ever since.

"In all this time, I don't think I've ever heard you say a negative word about anyone. Not even Dr. Haughty. So either you keep a lot bottled up — a whole *lot* bottled up — or you're an angel, sent to earth to set a good example for the rest of us run-of-the-mill grumblers."

Memory of all the mean-spirited things she'd called Reece in the privacy of her own mind made Taylor's mouth go dry. "Believe me," she said, taking a sip of tea, "I'm no angel."

"Mmm-hmm. And chickens have lips." She waved Taylor's denial away. "The way you took care of Mark when he got sick? Twenty-four-seven for months on end, without a break *or* a complaint? And let's not forget the way you wait on your guests, no matter how bad-mannered or ungrateful they are. And how you make time to volunteer at the kids' cancer center. And the —"

She'd heard it all before, from Eliot and Margo before they died, from her grandparents, Tootie and Isaac, even Mark's best friend Jimmy. Frankly, she'd grown tired of defending her decision to live by the Golden

71

Rule. It's what God expected of everyone, right, so why was *her* behavior viewed as something weird?

"Where's Isaac?"

Tootie shrugged. "Still in the barn, I'd guess."

"Good. I want the horses ready in case Jimmy wants to go riding when he gets here." *Please God,* she prayed, *let there be time for me to go with him.* Because oh, how she longed for a good hard ride on her dependable mare.

"Speaking of Jimmy, shouldn't he be here by now?"

Now Taylor shrugged, remembering how tired he'd sounded during their phone call last night. "Some problem with his tour bus. Said he'd leave as soon as he lined up the repairs. I'm guessing he won't be here before tomorrow at noon."

"Excellent! That means he'll be here when Dr. Haughty brings Eli home on Sunday night . . . give him a chance to see how a *real* man treats people."

"Tootie. . . ."

"Okay. All right. I can take a hint." She held up her hands. "No more badmouthing Dr. Thinks-He-Hung-the-Moon."

And chickens have lips, Taylor quoted silently.

"So how long is our favorite country singer staying this time?"

"Ten days." Jimmy had said that he wanted to fine-tune a few older songs and finesse a brand new one before he went back to his recording studio.

Tootie leaned back in her chair. "Oh, wow. A new song. What do you bet it's about you . . . again?"

Taylor only sighed.

"If he doesn't make a move on you this time, I'll eat my hat."

Taylor had tired of this conversation, too. "You aren't wearing a hat. In fact, I've never seen you in a hat. Do you even *own* one?"

"No, unless you count that knotty knitted mess I wear to shovel snow. But so what. I can always borrow Jimmy's ten-galloner. Or Dr. Haughty's know-it-all cap."

Sometimes, Taylor wished it was in her nature to say something like *Back off, Tootie!* or *Put a lid on it, will you!* Instead, Taylor bit her lip and covered the cookie plate with a blue gingham towel. "Jimmy is a friend. That's all he's ever been, all he'll ever —"

"C'mon, Taylor. We're BFFs. You can be honest with me."

"I *am* being honest with —"

Tootie counted on her fingers: "One, he practically owns that gorgeous island off the

Gulf Coast. Two, he's got a fully-staffed yacht. Three, every time we see a picture of him, he's posing with one of his Hollywood pals . . . and looking miserable as miserable can be. Four, he could afford to spend months in Europe or Tahiti or anyplace else in the world, but where does he go when he has time?"

Here.

"Now seriously, girlfriend, tell me why would a guy like that reserve an entire B&B, over and over for weeks on end, unless he's sweet on the innkeeper?"

She had to admit, the thought had crossed her mind a time or two. But she'd dismissed it. Jimmy was rich and famous, and could have his pick of Hollywood starlets and up-and-coming girl singers. What did he want with her!

"He comes here for peace and quiet and privacy, to work on his —"

"Pah! You might be able to convince me that he's just a friend, *if* he booked concerts in Blacksburg or Roanoke or someplace close. You know, to make the long stopovers here worth his time and money. Or if he brought a lady friend with him now and then."

"Jimmy works hard, touring the country, going overseas to entertain the troops. He'd have to entertain a lady friend, instead of settling in to —"

"Uh-huh. And those chickens wear *lipstick.*"

"He misses Mark almost as much as I do."

"Oh. Right. It's clear as glass now: he misses Mark. *That's* why every last one of his top-ten hits is all about unrequited love. And why every four months, he puts his career — correction — puts his entire *life* on hold, to spend two weeks in the middle of nowhere to write another one here at the Misty Wolf."

Taylor exhaled a sigh of frustration. She supposed all this protective stuff was proof that Tootie meant it when she said, "I love you like a sister!" Then . . . why couldn't her "sister" see how uncomfortable things like this made her?

"Look, I know it's none of my business," Tootie said, standing, "but how else can you explain that he leaves a stable full of thoroughbreds on his fancy Nashville ranch to ride your bad-tempered dapple grays?"

"They aren't bad-tempered . . . if you know how to handle them."

"How big is that quilt of yours gonna be, if you don't mind my asking?"

She didn't mind at all, especially considering it changed the subject. "Oh, I don't know. I'm guessing big enough for a full-sized bed?"

"Then it looks like you have a lot of sewing left to do. Why not use the machine, instead of hand-stitching it?"

"Because most of the pieces of fabric are old. I don't want to risk pulling a thread." And besides, she thought, it'll feel good knowing that I finished every single stitch exactly the way Mom would have. . . .

"See ya later . . . Artful *Do-o*-odger-r-r," Tootie sang.

Taylor put down her quilting and followed Tootie onto the porch. How like her to get in a parting shot, and then high-tail it out the door! "Just because I can't explain the whole Jimmy thing doesn't mean I'm dodging anything. Mark was Jimmy's drummer, and they worked together nearly every day for years. They were closer than most brothers. A few days before Mark died, I heard him ask Jimmy to check in on me from time to time. If anything, he's using the visits to keep that promise to Mark."

Tootie threw a leg over her bike seat. "Do me a favor, will you?"

"Anything . . . unless it's Jimmy-related."

"Pay attention to the way he looks at you. I mean, *really* pay attention, okay?"

He would look at her the way he always

had . . . as his best friend's widow. "I hate to sound like a nag, but that's Jimmy-related."

"Yeah, well," she said, nudging up the kickstand, "some things just have to be said."

"Oh, really. And why is that?"

"Because you're the only one who can't see that he's crazy about you. If you ask me, it's kinda mean-spirited to string him along."

"String him along? Holy mackerel, Tootie, that's just . . . well, that's just plain *silly* is what it is! You're the one who's always saying that with his good looks and talent, all he'd have to do is snap his fingers and a parade of beauties would line up to audition for the role of Mrs. Jimmy Jacobs. What would a guy like that want with *me*?"

"You're impossible," she said, rolling forward, "but I love you like a sister. Even if you are stubborn as a mule." The ten speed *tick-tick-ticked* as it carried her toward the road. "See you in the morning," she called over her shoulder.

"Oh, fine," Taylor whispered, "I'm stubborn because I don't agree with you?"

"Mark my words," Tootie hollered, "if you'll just *look,* you'll see that I'm right!"

Oh, she'd look, all right.

The only question, really, was whether Tootie would prefer salt and pepper or hot sauce when she made good on her bet to eat Jimmy's Stetson!

4

After tossing and turning for hours, Taylor decided to make one more check of the suite Jimmy would call home for the next ten days. Unfortunately, she'd made one last check so many times before turning in that not so much as a speck of dust had settled on the gleaming mahogany furnishings.

So she checked the rest of the guest rooms and all five attached baths. The library. The parlor and the dining room. And finally, the sun porch. It hardly seemed possible that in a house this size, she couldn't find a single chore to take her mind off the bothersome notions Tootie had planted in her brain, not the least of which was Reece's limp. While Margo was alive, Taylor might have had a chance to find out if injury or birth defect caused it, if it caused him pain. In the ten or so years since they'd met, he'd never mentioned it, so expecting the subject to come up during an everyday conversation wasn't likely. "Well, Tootie," she said to herself, " 'whiner' sure isn't something you can add to your list of insults!"

The grandfather clock in the front hall announced the five o'clock hour, startling her. Just last week, one of her guests — a self-professed clockmaker — spent the better part of an hour explaining how she could silence the chime between 10:00 p.m. and 6:00 a.m. She appreciated the subtlety of his complaint — his hadn't been the first — and to show her gratitude, sent him and his wife on their way with a fully stocked picnic basket, free of charge. She'd had every good intention of following up on his suggestion, but a wind storm loosened some shingles on the chicken coop roof, and a rotting tree near the road had fallen onto the paddock gate, forcing her penciled "buy clock parts" to the end of her to-do list . . . already sixteen items long.

With the storm little more than a blustery memory, she made quick work of replacing the shingles, and the logs Isaac stacked after cleaning up tree debris would assure plenty of firewood to feed the parlor woodstove this winter. It felt good, hearing the weatherman predict three days of sunshine, because Jimmy had never been fond of cloudy skies.

She'd still been hard at work on the quilt when the clock struck three. Few things annoyed her more than leaving a task unfinished, but she'd nodded off while stitching a scrap of Margo's cheerleading uniform to Eliot's flannel shirt. Though that finger-prick to the thumb hadn't stained the material, it seemed best to quit.

"Might as well enjoy a cup of tea," she whispered, "since there's nothing else to do." Grabbing a mug from the cupboard, Taylor remembered her earlier conversation with Tootie. If she truly believed her own words — that Jimmy's feelings for her were strictly platonic — what difference did today's forecast make? Should the weather turn, he'd find ways to brighten a cloudy day, just like any other guest.

Right?

She poured steaming water over a teabag, and eyes closed, inhaled the scent of spicy peaches. Like it or not, there was nothing "just" when it came to Jimmy. He'd been like a brother to Mark, and over the years, had become a dear friend to her, too.

Taylor sat at the table and opened the most recent issue of the *New River Valley* magazine. She'd held a subscription for years, mostly so that her guests could peruse the colorful pages to find nearby sights and activities to fill their days at the Misty Wolf. Seeing to their needs meant that she rarely had time to read it herself. Restaurant reviews, profiles of local artisans, recipes that featured produce grown in the area, and an article explaining the ups and downs of the stock market kept her reading until her cup was empty.

She checked the time and groaned. "Oh, great," she muttered, scribbling "Change battery in kitchen clock" at the bottom of her to-do list. The glowing numerals on the microwave matched the ones above the stove, but not the ones on the clock. "Good thing I can count on you guys for accuracy."

And then she chuckled under her breath. Good thing there were no guests around to hear her talking to herself, or they'd pack up so fast, all she'd see was the blur of their cars, speeding down the drive. Either that, or the Misty Wolf would attract a whole new type of visitors — the kind who were attracted to ghosts and goblins and crazy innkeepers.

"Maybe you should get a cat," she told herself. As she refilled her mug, Taylor added "At least then if anybody catches you talking to yourself, you could always say you were talking to the —"

"Funny. I always figured you for a dog lover."

Taylor spun around so fast that she sloshed hot tea all over her white socks. "Good grief, Jimmy," she sputtered, free hand pressed over her hammering heart, "you just shaved the last ten years off my life!"

"Way I hear it, those are the worst ten years, anyway, so I guess you owe me one for sparing you that."

As he put down his guitar case and hung his Stetson on the hook behind the door, Taylor wondered how he'd managed to get here hours ahead of schedule . . . and into the kitchen without a key. And did his warm hello hug feel slightly tighter, last a little longer than usual, or did it just seem that way because of everything Tootie had said?

"You look great," he said, holding her at arm's length.

Instinct made her run a hand through her curls. She hadn't brushed her hair — or her teeth — since heading up to bed last night. Fingertips over her mouth, she put one white-socked foot atop the other and thanked God that the hem of Mark's old denim shirt hung past her knees.

Stepping back, Jimmy pointed, first at the coffee maker, then at her mug. "Is your cof-

83

fee pot broken?"

"No, but I didn't see much point in brewing a whole pot, just for me."

"That's good, 'cause I don't know what I'd do if you went over to the other side."

"What other side?"

"You know . . ." He held one pinky aloft. "Traded your coffee addiction for tea?" Laughing, he leaned his backside against the sink. Arms folded across his chest, he added, "You need to take that TV commercial a little more seriously."

"What commercial?"

"You know, the one where the beautiful woman says 'I'm worth it.' "

She giggled because he looked even sillier than he sounded, trying to imitate the actress's posture and voice. "Is that your understated way of saying you'd like a cup, right now?"

"Understated," he quoted, one eye narrowed as he tapped his bristled chin. "Now there's a word that's never been used to describe me."

Taylor filled the carafe with water, and emptied it into the reservoir. "So enlighten me, O understated one, when did you start wearing the five o'clock shadow all the movie stars and singers are sporting these days?"

Jimmy shrugged one shoulder. "When you mow the lawn, you don't go clean down to the dirt, do you?"

She thought about that for a minute. "No, I guess not, but —"

"I drove straight through, so I'm whipped, but I'm not *that* tired."

She hit the On button and faced him.

He winked. "You think I didn't notice how you shifted the focus from you to me?"

"I hate to admit it, but I don't have a clue what you're talking about."

"Mmm-hmm."

He said it a little too knowingly for Taylor's taste, but she didn't dare admit it. Out loud, anyway.

"The commercial, remember, where the girl says she's worth it? The gist of it being, why not give *Taylor* the TLC she deserves, at least once in a while?" He nodded at the coffee pot. "If you want a cup, then perk it, even if it means you'll pour the second one right down the drain, because . . ."

" 'You're worth it,' " she quoted. He'd said things like that before. Everybody in her life, it seemed, had said things like that before! She could feel him watching as she arranged a mug, the sugar and milk, and a spoon on the placemat nearest him. If Jimmy — and the rest of them — knew how

many ways she'd let down the people closest to her, they'd sing another tune.

"I didn't expect you until tomorrow, at
the earliest. How'd you manage to get away
so early?"

When his left brow rise slightly, she half
expected him to adopt Tootie's "You're the
Artful Dodger" attitude. Instead, Jimmy
said, "I gave Cory a bonus, put him in
charge of the bus."

"The bus? What's wrong with it?"

"Nothing serious. Fuel pump, I think."
He shrugged. "Cory's better at that kind of
stuff than I am anyway," he said as she put
the mugs on the table. "And with another
kid on the way, I figure he can use the extra
money. Plus, it keeps him close to home."

His tone made her look up, and it surprised her to see that his expression was
even grimmer than his voice. Shouldn't this
be *good* news? "That's wonderful! What
does this make for him and Julie . . . four?"

"Uh-huh." Jimmy shook his head and
pointed. "I think we should contact the
Guinness people about that coffee pot of
yours."

She perked coffee in a big, shiny urn on
mornings when the inn was all booked up.
When it wasn't, Taylor had the same complaint about this one: it gave new meaning

to the word slow.

And then it dawned on her that Jimmy had been here five minutes without a single reference to Eli. That wasn't like him. And . . . had he deliberately changed the subject from Cory's growing family to sluggish coffeemakers, or did it just seem that way?

"Wasn't very smart, driving straight through from L.A. to Blacksburg. What did it take you . . . twenty, thirty hours?"

"Close."

No doubt he'd encountered traffic jams, road construction, bad weather, or all three. No wonder he didn't seem his usual fun-loving self! "Guess it's a good thing," she said, handing him a mug, "that I used decaffeinated grounds, huh?"

"Why?"

"Because you look like something my nonexistent cat might have dragged in, that's why, and high-test would only keep you from falling asleep quickly and getting the rest you need."

"Gee, if the Guinness book has a 'Good for a Guy's Ego' category, you're *in* like Flynn, Bradley!"

It wasn't like him to pout. Wasn't like him to call her by her last name either. "Now, now, you know I didn't mean it that way.

You look as handsome as ever, just a little tired and rough around the —"

"Even days on the road and more than two thousand miles?" Chuckling, he puffed out his chest.

Her guests rarely had to ask for anything, from second helpings to extra amenities for their rooms, because she'd learned to read their faces, their voices and posture; anticipating and providing what they needed kept them coming back year after year and recommending the Misty Wolf to friends and family. Right now, she read Jimmy's expression as hopeful.

But hopeful about *what*? Had Tootie been right?

"More than two thousand miles," she echoed. "Did you get any sleep?"

"Aw, now," he drawled, "don't worry your pretty li'l head. I squeaked in a few hours here and there."

Where, she started to ask, on the side of the road? But Tootie's warning stopped her. "Well, you're here now, safe and sound. That's all that matters."

Something between affection and appreciation glowed in his eyes. "And I'd bet my next contract that my room is ready and waiting, and exactly the way I like it."

"If I've forgotten anything," she said, "I

expect you to tell me." Eyes narrowed, she aimed her pointer finger in his direction. "Got it?"

"Yes, ma'am."

She pulled out a chair — the very one Reece had chosen hours ago — and invited him to sit. Thankfully, Jimmy had never been a fussy guest, like the ones who insisted on Starbucks' coffee or eiderdown pillows. It had been quite by accident that she'd learned about his allergies to her brand of fabric softener; the fact that he would have put up with the itchy rash rather than complain or put her to any extra trouble made her want to take *better* care of him. As he stirred milk into his coffee, Taylor said, "Hungry?"

"Matter of fact, I'm starving." He rubbed his palms together. "Know what I've been thinking about for the past couple hundred miles?"

Taylor opened the fridge. "Let me guess," she said, grabbing the egg carton, "two over easy with a side order of scrapple — good 'n' crisp — and wheat toast slathered with apple butter."

She was cutting into the scrapple package when he said, "Guess you're wondering about the real reason I got here so early."

"Actually," she said, slicing it into ten tidy

servings, "the better question is how you got *in* here."

Jimmy laughed. "You gave me a key years ago. Remember, when . . ."

Taylor didn't need to ask why he'd stopped talking so abruptly, because yes, she remembered: that sticky summer the night before Mark died, he'd asked her to call Jimmy, who canceled his concert and rushed from Atlanta to Blacksburg. And because it had been so last-minute, he'd been forced to bring his dog, so she'd given him the key so that he could leave Rufus at the Misty Wolf.

"Don't mind me," she said, turning up the fire under the frying pan. "I get a little fuzzy-brained when I pull all-nighters."

"I hope you didn't do that on my account. Because I haven't always had live-in help. I remember how to make up a bed, you know."

His quiet comment reminded her of the way Jimmy held her hand as she finalized the funeral arrangements, then insisted that she try to catch a short nap. She never expected to sleep, but those grueling hours surrounding Mark's death must have taken more out of her than she'd realized. When she woke up four hours later, Isaac and Tootie told her how he'd fed the last of her guests, gathered up all the towels and bed linens and readied every room for the next guests before scribbling a note that instructed her to call him any time she needed to talk. The few times she'd been tempted to pick up the phone, she'd immersed herself in work, instead, the way she always had when facing heartache or difficulty or —

Jimmy put two slices of bread into the toaster. "I hope you're not gonna make me eat alone."

She shrugged off the memories and concentrated on the fact that the meal wasn't just Jimmy's favorite, it was hers, too. Besides, she hadn't had a bite since lunch, yesterday. "You know, I *am* hungry."

He added two more slices, then went to the fridge. "So what's on your schedule this morning?" he asked, taking the apple butter from a shelf in the door.

"I need to go into town for a few things."

"Mind if I saddle up ol' Millie and take a ride while you're gone?"

"She'd love that. Isaac got everything ready for you yesterday."

He opened and closed a few cabinet doors. "Ah, there they are," he said, sliding two plates from the top of the stack. "Maybe Isaac will want to ride along."

Not likely, Taylor thought; the man rarely

went anywhere that put a mile or an hour between himself and Tootie. "Can't hurt to ask," Taylor said, pouring a mound of flour onto the cutting board.

Now he opened and closed drawers, and finding the one with the silverware in it, said, "Has that old buzzard popped the question yet?"

She stopped whipping eggs long enough to glance over at him. "Didn't realize he was considering it."

"Well, color me surprised. I thought he told you *every*thing."

"Evidently not."

With the table already set and the toaster ready to go, Jimmy leaned his backside against the counter again, this time, right next to Taylor's workspace. "This is nice," he said, nodding. "You. Me. Talking. Making breakfast together . . ."

Smiling, Taylor dipped scrapple slices into the beaten egg, then into the flour.

". . . like an old married couple."

Now why had he felt the need to tack on *that* particular postscript? "So how many unfinished melodies did you bring with you this time?"

He took a sideways step farther from her. "Not many. Two, maybe three."

Just that quickly, his voice had gone from

relaxed to tense. Taylor hadn't meant to hurt his feelings, but she couldn't very well let him continue with that line of conversation and expect things to remain strictly platonic between them.

"You'll find four different types of juice in the fridge. If you're pouring, I'll have —"

"Tomato. I know." He grabbed two small glasses from the cupboard behind his head and put them at the two o'clock position beside each of their plates. "So what's up with the sewing basket?" he asked, pointing to where it stood near the heavy swinging door that led into the dining room.

"Oh. That." She placed the battered scrapple slices into hot oil, and as they sizzled, she told him how Eli had talked her into going up into the attic, where she'd found her mother's unfinished quilt in an old trunk. "I'm going to add to it, a story behind each square, so he'll have something to remember Eliot and Margo by."

He'd filled one glass halfway, and stopped midstream. "That's just about the most thoughtful thing I've ever heard." Jimmy put the juice back into the fridge and tapped a fingertip to the quilt design she'd sketched and taped to the freezer door. "Looks like a lot of work," he said, moving back to the toaster. "I know Eli has been through a lot, but he's some lucky kid, having someone like you looking out for him."

"No, I'm the lucky one," she admitted. "He's improved my life in every imaginable way."

Jimmy harrumphed. "Think how much more you'd enjoy him if you didn't have to share him with that cantankerous uncle of his."

He'd only met Reece in passing, so what right did he have to say *uncle* as if it were a curse word? And then, she remembered the muggy summer night when Reece picked Eli up for their first official weekend together. She and Eli had been nearly inseparable those first two months prior, redecorating his room, getting him registered in school and at church, prowling the grounds and house so that he'd know his way around and *believe* the Misty Wolf was every bit as much his as it was hers. She'd held it together as Eli hugged her good-bye, as Reece wordlessly buckled him into the booster seat, as his shiny black car roared down the driveway. It wasn't until that final turn took it out of sight that she turned into a blubbering, sniffling mess.

"What a rude, ungrateful jerk!" Jimmy had barked. "If you hadn't gone to bat for him, he wouldn't even *have* every-other-weekend visits." Eyes narrowed, he'd pulled her into a protective hug and turned her tears into giggles by saying "Want me to punch his lights out?"

Back then, she'd believed the hug had been brotherly and the threat, just a bad joke. Now, she wasn't so sure.

Jimmy carried the saucer of toast to the table and sat down. Taylor held the plate of eggs in one hand, scrapple in the other, and decided this was as good a time as any to set the record straight. "I'm so lucky to have a friend like you," she said, meaning it.

Jimmy looked at her for a long, quiet moment, and then he sighed. "You gonna hog all that scrapple, or can I have a slice?"

5

It had taken *hours,* but Taylor found everything on her list, from the foldaway cutting
mat to milliner needles and basting pins,
shiny new thimbles and thread, and a brand
new pair of guaranteed-not-to-slip-or-snag
scissors. "Decisions, decisions," she
mumbled as the Next Door Bake Shop
entrance came into view. The cafe served
her favorite beverage — coconut latte —
and its Thai-born owner had a flair for baking cookies and muffins even more tasty
than her own. What better place to rest up
after a long morning of shopping for quilt
supplies!

Aivey waved as she lugged her cache up
to the counter. "Hey, Taylor! How are you
today?"

"I'm fine, and I'll be even better if you tell
me you made fresh fudge macaroons and
pumpkin muffins today."

"You are in luck!" she said over the din of

giggling kids and their moms. "Two dozen of each, as usual?"

"Better make it one," she said, patting her stomach. "I only have one guest this weekend, and he isn't nearly as sweet on sweets as I am!"

Dark eyes glittering with mischief, Aivey grinned. "Ah, so this must mean your Jimmy Jacobs is in town."

"Yep, he arrived early this morning." And since even Aivey was saying things like "*her* Jimmy," it was probably best not to tell her *how* early.

Aivey grabbed an empty box from the shelf. "And how long will he stay with you *this* time?" she asked, eyebrows wiggling as she filled it with muffins.

"A week, maybe more." Evidently, Tootie had been singing the "Taylor and Jimmy, sittin' in a tree" song in Blacksburg, not just around the inn. "And I know it's nearly lunchtime, so if you can spare it, could you add a quart of your mushroom-barley soup to the order?"

While Aivey taped up the muffin box, she nodded at the cutting mat, peeking from one of the bags scattered at Taylor's feet. "Are you making so many quilts for your Misty Wolf Inn that you have worn out the old one?"

"No," Taylor said, laughing, "I just needed something I could fold up fast, so I don't have to pack everything up when I try to hide my latest project. The quilt I'm working on now is a special surprise, for Eli."

"Ah, you must have been wishing to see him, then," Aivey said with a nod toward the door.

Taylor turned, and sure enough, there was Eli, pulling and tugging at the handle of the big glass door as his proud-faced uncle pretended *not* to want to help him open it.

Aivey leaned forward to whisper "Last time your Eli was here, he told me that he asks to eat breakfast here at the shop *every* time he is in town." She ladled soup into a round carton. "But too bad for Eli," she added, tamping its lid into place, "the doctor, he insists on making pancakes."

Taylor knew a few bachelor dads, and every last one of them took shortcuts. Especially where food was concerned. Pizzas and subs, pre-packaged foods, TV dinners and fast food. She thought it was wonderful that Reece took the time and trouble to prepare healthy, home-cooked meals when Eli was with him.

"He is a very polite little boy. Too polite to tell Dr. Montgomery that he is not very good at pancakes."

Eli spotted Taylor just then, and raced to the counter. "Taylor!" he shouted, throwing his arms around her waist. "What're you doing all the way over here?"

"Oh, just running a few errands."

Aivey wiggled her pointer finger. "Oh, Eli," she said, "look what I have for you."

"Cookie crumblers? Yay!"

While Eli munched, Reece sent Taylor a hello nod. "Good to see you."

Then why the frown? she wondered. "You, too." She blamed the sunshine, pouring through the big gleaming windows. Better that than think sharing Eli — even for a few minutes during one of *his* weekends — had put it there.

He nodded again, this time at her shopping bags. "Did you leave anything for the rest of Blacksburg?"

What's this, she thought, a smile *and* a joke from the ever-somber Dr. Montgomery? But before she could reply, Aivey put the boxes on the counter and handed her a sales receipt. "Thank you, Taylor. I hope your guest will enjoy the soup *and* the treats!"

"Guest?" Eli asked. "I thought nobody was staying with us until —" He clasped both hands under his chin, as if praying. "Oh, wow . . . did Jimmy get here early?"

99

Without even thinking, she plucked a napkin from the basket on the counter and dusted cookie crumbs from one corner of his mouth. "He arrived this morning," she said, dabbing at the other side.

"Way cool! That means he'll be there when I get home tomorrow night, right?"

"Yes, he'll be there."

Reece slapped a hand to the back of his neck. Taylor couldn't be sure, but she thought he might have groaned softly, too. Not that she blamed him. It had to smart a little, hearing Eli's excitement, especially knowing the boy would spend more time with Jimmy in the coming days than with his uncle. She could tell him that if this visit went the way others had, Jimmy would put in more hours with his guitar than with Eli. Better still, she could invite Reece to dinner one night next week, to see for himself.

"So did you guys see the dolphin movie last night?"

"We sure did!" While Eli launched into a detailed retelling of the plot, Taylor led him to a table. Without skipping a beat, he sat down and, thankfully, so did Reece, because the three of them were causing quite a stir in the little cafe. When the boy finally took a breath, Taylor laughed. "My *good*ness! I'm positively green with envy. You didn't get anywhere near this excited about that old Chipmunks movie that I took you to see!"

It was the right thing to say, she realized when a slow, grateful smile lit Reece's face.

He tapped his wristwatch. "It's nearly lunchtime. What would you say to joining us for soup and a sandwich?"

Much as she wanted to say yes, Taylor didn't feel right about horning in on his time with Eli.

"Jimmy," Reece said, misunderstanding her hesitation, "is a grown man. I'm sure he can take care of himself for an hour or two."

"Oh, no he can't!" Eli blurted. "He almost cutted off his finger once, trying to carve a Thanksgiving turkey. 'Member, Taylor?"

Yes, now that he'd mentioned it, she did remember. Odd, though, that she'd put it out of her mind, considering it was her first Thanksgiving without Mark.

She read the confusion in Reece's eyes as he tried to remember the event. "That was the year you were visiting your folks in Africa, remember?"

"Not really." His frown intensified. "It isn't easy, keeping track of my globetrotting missionary parents."

She pretended not to notice the cynicism in his voice. "They were in Zimbabwe, weren't they? And I think you joined them to vaccinate the mission kids."

"Yeah, that's right." The look on his face said what words needn't: *the year when your pigheaded brother signed up for another tour of duty in Iraq, and started the bad news dominos tumbling.*

In Taylor's opinion, his sister's reaction to Eliot's deployment had been just as pigheaded. Margo had holed up in her bedroom, and if Eli hadn't begged her to get out of the house, well, there wouldn't have *been* a Thanksgiving dinner that year. A good thing, as it turned out, because no doubt she'd have spent the entire weekend nursing a hefty case of lonely widow pity. Instead, she'd invited everyone without a better place to go to join them, including Jimmy and half of his band and their families.

"I don't think I ever saw more blood than that," Eli said, grimacing at the memory.

The image was just as clear in Taylor's mind: Jimmy, so busy scratching his bedbug-induced rash, that he nearly severed an artery with the carving knife. If he hadn't waited until the last minute to have his bus serviced, he could have spent the night in it. But he'd waited until the last minute to book a room, too, and ended up in the dilapidated motel on Highway 412.

"Nope," Eli added. "No way I trust that guy to make a sammich, not even if he used a butter knife, 'cause I sure don't want to spend another boring night in the boring hospital waiting room!"

If she didn't know better, Taylor might say Reece *enjoyed* hearing that the famous Jimmy Jacobs was such a procrastinating incompetent that he'd nearly lopped off his own hand.

He folded his hands on the table. "So what do you say? Will you join us for lunch?"

"Say yes, Taylor," Eli prodded. "It'll be fun!"

She wanted to say yes, but her packages were hogging up precious floor space. "And then there's the soup," she said, mostly to herself. "It really ought to be refrigerated."

"Hey," Eli piped up. "I have an idea. Uncle Reece keeps a cooler in the back seat for my juice boxes and chocolate milk and stuff." He beamed at his uncle. "Bet he'd let you borrow it . . . if you say please."

"Good plan, kiddo." Reece met Taylor's gaze to add, "I can stow your packages in your car. I mean, since I'll be out there, anyway, putting your soup into the cooler. If you'll join us, that is." He held out one hand, palm up. "And if you'll give me your keys." Grinning, he looked at Eli and winked. "Please?"

It did sound like fun. And she hadn't eaten since sunrise. Unshouldering her purse, Taylor searched for her key ring. "My car is parked right —"

"Across the street," Reece finished for her. "We know. Li'l eagle eyes, here, spotted it on our way in."

She handed him the keys. "But I have to warn you, the remote thingy is so old that the symbols have worn off. The button on the right is the horn, and the left one unlocks the doors." She was about to add, *or is it the other way around?* when her stomach growled. Loud enough that she hoped the cafe's chatter and clatter had camouflaged it.

No such luck, she realized when Eli said, "Are you hungry already?"

"Actually, I had a nice big breakfast." She didn't think it necessary to add *at five o'clock this morning.*

But she had *shared* that big breakfast with Jimmy, and she didn't want to risk adding fuel to the "he's your man" fire. "I'm fine. So what do you guys have planned for the rest of the afternoon?"

"Our idea man, here, says his teacher told him to . . ." He turned to Eli. "What's the assignment again?"

The boy hung his head and mumbled "Draw something about a place where I want to go but never did. Yet."

"So I thought we'd head over to Smith-field Plantation when we're through here," Reece continued. "Believe it or not, I've never been there, either, even though it's been right here under my nose for years. You're welcome to join us."

She thought of the quilt, still sitting in a heap on the kitchen table. What if Jimmy got it in his head to cook something, and stained it by accident, just because she'd forgotten to put it away? Besides, Mark had taken her to the plantation shortly before his cancer diagnosis. "Thanks, but I have a to-do list that's as long as my arm." She leaned closer to Eli. "When did Mrs. Cunningham give you this homework assignment?"

"What is the day before yesterday?"

"Thursday."

"Yeah. That's the one."

"And it's due when you go back to school on Monday?"

He put his chin on the table and made goofy faces at his reflection in the chrome napkin holder. "Uh-huh."

"I don't understand, Eli. You didn't have school on Friday. Why is this the first I'm hearing about your assignment?"

"Because," he droned, "you never let me do anything fun until my homework is done. And I thought and thought and I thought, but I couldn't think up a single place that I wanted to see." He looked adoringly at his uncle. "Then I thought 'Uncle Reece will think of something!' "

Taylor looked at Reece, too . . . just in time to see him wince.

"I, ah, I assumed that you knew about it," he explained, "and that letting me take charge was your way of saying 'do your share for a change.' "

A few weeks earlier, she'd started a campaign to teach Eli that even four-year-old boys needed to take some accountability for schoolwork and minor chores around the inn. Had he shared their discussions about responsibility and duty with Reece?

"I feel like a ninny, admitting this," she began, "but it never occurred to me that you'd want to help with spelling lessons and simple addition and show-and-tell. You're a pediatrician, for heaven's sake, surrounded by whiny kids all day long. Not that *Eli* is like that, of course. Unless you've asked him to print 'Eli Reece Bradley' in the spaces between the fat blue lines on those flimsy sheets of writing paper." She was rambling and knew it but couldn't seem to stop herself.

Reece smiled as he closed his right fist around her keys, grabbed the handles of her shopping bags with the left. "Might as well get this out of the way," he said. And using his chin as a pointer, he alerted Taylor to Eli's wide-eyed, guilty expression. "When I bring him home, maybe we can set a time to talk. You know, about things like homework and field trips and . . . stuff."

Taylor picked up a menu as he shouldered his way out of the cafe. "What are you in the mood for today, my little man? Panini? Pot pie? Chicken wrap?"

"Um-m-m. . . ."

No doubt he was wishing Aivey would add burgers, fries, and pizza to the menu. "I wonder what your Uncle Reece is in the mood for?"

"He always gets the chicken wrap, so —"

The nonstop beeping of a car horn interrupted him. *Her* car horn.

"Uh-oh," Eli said, looking toward the windows.

"You recognize it, too, do you?"

He got onto his knees for a better look, then faced her and grinned. "Guess the *right* button was the *wrong* one, huh."

Lord help me, I'm raising a comedian.

And then, the blessed relief of silence that told her Reece had figured out — and corrected — her mistake. A moment later, he sat across from her, wearing a grin that matched Eli's, right down to the puckish dimple in his right cheek.

She wasn't sure what he'd order, or what they'd talk about over soup and sandwiches, but one thing was certain . . .

. . . lunch would *not* be boring.

6

"Lunch was delicious, and I'm stuffed!" Taylor said. "But really, I wish you had let me pick up the check. I couldn't have stayed if not for the loan of the cooler. And then there's the matter of my car's horn almost deafening you."

He screwed a fingertip into his ear. "Sorry, come again?"

Her eyes grew big and round, and when she got the joke, what followed wasn't a tinny giggle, like Dixie's, but a happy, hearty laugh that turned heads . . . and his heart.

"Next time," he said, opening the driver's door, "lunch is on you."

She squatted to make herself kid-sized — not that she had far to go, tiny as she was — and wrapped Eli in a hug every bit as hearty as her laugh. Her vibrant calf-length skirt formed a gauzy puddle around them, and for a minute there, Reece found himself wishing *he* could join them in the colorful arc.

"Have fun at the plantation," she said, kissing the tip of his nose, "and I'll see you tomorrow." When she straightened, Taylor faced Reece. "See you tomorrow, too. Maybe you can read him a bedtime story and listen to his prayers, and afterward, we'll go over his schedule . . . and stuff." She bit her lower lip. "Unless you already have other plans, that is."

"It's either Eli's schedule or balance my checkbook."

"I'll make a light snack of some sort . . . sherbet, maybe, or —"

"Do I get to stay up late and have some?" Eli wanted to know.

And Taylor said, "We couldn't eat your favorite dessert without including you, now could we?"

When she laughed, her dangly silver earrings caught a shard of sunlight. Even they didn't sparkle nearly as much as her eyes. Reece remembered the night when, to save time before seeing a play in town, he had picked Dixie up on his way back to the Misty Wolf. He'd introduced Taylor to his fiancée, who remarked during the drive to the theater that Taylor had probably kept Maybelline in business: "I'll bet it takes a whole tube of mascara to make her eyelashes look that long and thick." But standing here in the bright sunlight, it was easy to see how wrong Dixie had been, about the makeup . . . and a whole lot of other things that had nothing to do with Taylor.

She tossed her enormous purse onto the passenger seat, and as she started to slide in behind the steering wheel, caught her heel in the hem of her skirt. It threw her off balance, and if he hadn't wrapped both hands around her waist, she'd have toppled face-first into the gutter.

"Can you believe it? What a total klutz I am!" Blinking up into his face, she added "If you hadn't been here, I would have ended up *there.*" She steadied herself by planting both hands on his chest, using her chin to point at the mini-river of black water, fed by last night's storm, that carried soda straws and cigarette butts toward the manhole down the block.

"That wouldn't have been good," he said, surprised by the gravelly tone of his voice. He got a whiff of her shampoo — the same flowery scent he'd inhaled in the lawyer's office when she'd leaned over to suggest weekend visits with Eli. He could have kissed her, because the proposal had taken the sting out of learning that Margo left him nothing but the mortgage on a house that wasn't even his.

Taylor was close enough to kiss now, too, and the realization set his heart to hammering. She must have felt it pounding like a parade drum, because she stepped back, leaving two cold spots where her warm little palms had been.

"If you like," she said, easing into the car, "I can fix supper for you and Eli on Sunday, too."

It crossed his mind as he stood, one hand on the seat's headrest, the other atop the open door, that she could read his mind. Because this time when he acknowledged that he was close enough to kiss her, she licked her lips.

"We were gonna eat the Tay-getti that you made for us for Sunday dinner," Eli said from somewhere behind Reece.

"We could bring it," Reece said, "and heat it up at your place."

Taylor leaned forward, just enough to see around Reece's bulk. "No, sweetie, the spaghetti was supposed to be a guys-only meal. Besides," she said, turning the key in the ignition, "now we're even."

"Even?"

"I've got one of your coolers," she said, aiming a thumb over her shoulder, "and

112

you've got one of mine."

"Ah," he said, closing the door. "Drive safely, and we'll see you tomorrow."

Eli stepped up to the open window. "What were you *gonna* fix for supper, before I got all stupid and reminded you about leftovers?"

"To be honest, I have no idea!"

All three of them shared a moment of laughter. A good sound, Reece thought as she shifted into drive.

She pressed a kiss to her fingertips, then blew it toward Eli . . . and he pretended to catch it. Then she pointed at her heart, at him, and drove away.

Reece didn't know how long he'd stood there, watching her car get smaller and smaller. It took Eli, tugging at his hand, to make him aware that he'd been staring, openmouthed, like an addle-brained boy in the throes of his first crush.

"Well," he said, "are you ready, li'l buddy?"

Eli's shoulders sagged and he exhaled a heavy sigh. "I've *been* ready. It was you two, lookin' all googly-eyed at each other that held us up."

"Googly-eyed, huh?" he said as they walked hand in hand toward the car.

"Oh, yeah. Big time."

"Where'd you even hear such an old-fashioned word?"

Eli shrugged. "I dunno. A cartoon, or maybe one of those black-and-white movies Taylor likes to watch after I go to bed."

The picture of her, curled up on the couch — a bowl of popcorn in her lap and dabbing a tissue to the corner of her eye as *Wuthering Heights* or *Destry Rides Again* flickered on the screen — distracted him so much that he almost didn't think to ask how Eli knew what was on TV.

Before he could pose the question, Eli tugged at his elbow. "Um, Uncle Reece?" he asked, "you gonna unlock the door?"

"Sorry, buddy," he said, opening it.

Eli buckled his seatbelt, and waited for Reece to buckle his to say, "If you like her so much, why don't you just marry her?"

Surely Eli was kidding. Reece could find out for sure, with nothing more than a quick glance in the rearview mirror. But he fired up the engine, instead, because how would he respond to wide-eyed proof that the boy had been 100 percent serious?

"Sure would make life easier for everybody. No more packing and unpacking. No more driving back and forth. No more mix-ups over homework and stuff."

Shaking his head, Reece blended into the

traffic on Turner Street. *How old are you really, Eli,* he wondered, risking a peek in the mirror. *Forty? Fifty-five?* Because he didn't know another four-year-old with the capacity to figure stuff like that out, let alone articulate it! He'd share the story with Taylor when he dropped Eli off tomorrow . . . if there was a way to do it without letting her know about the crazy thoughts clanging in his own brain.

Several times as they rode down Route 412, Eli hollered out "Punch buggy blue!" and "Purple tractor trailer!" It was a game Reece invented to help pass the time between his place in town and the Misty Wolf. Thankfully, it was holding Eli's attention today.

"Look! There's Buffalo Wild Wings!" he said as they made the left onto 460. "We haven't gone there in a *long,* long time."

And it was true. Knowing how talented Taylor was in the kitchen, he'd made a point of trying to cook for Eli, too. But maybe a steady diet of home-cooked meals was precisely why the boy enjoyed eating out, at least once in a while. "Next visit," Reece promised. Then, "You up for a little navigating?"

"Sure!" He sat up as straight as the straps of the booster seat would allow. "What am I looking for this time?"

"Maywood Street. It'll be our signal for the next turn."

"How is it spelled?"

No sooner did Reece answer than Eli belted out "I see it, I see it!"

"Yep, and now watch for Coal Bank Hollow." He spelled that, too.

"Now what?" he asked as Reece made the turn.

"Batts Road."

When the sign came into view, Eli read "B-A-T-T-S." And pointing, he added, "1-7-7-3. Is that the address?"

"No, it's the year William Preston moved there."

He thought about it for a minute before asking, "Then why isn't it called Preston Plantation?"

"Because his wife's name was Smith before she married him."

"I still don't get it."

Reece chuckled. The couple had six kids by the time Preston bought the land, but Eli would learn that soon enough. He hoped the tour, itself, would clear things up . . . and hold the boy's interest.

His concerns were quickly alleviated as he watched Eli, listening intently to every word their guide said. Eli asked dozens of questions, from how things were made "in the old days" to which tools were used to make them, and seemed particularly fascinated by the construction of the rough-hewn wood fence that surrounded the garden.

When the tour ended, he noticed the gift shop. "Is it like the one at the rock museum?"

As they walked toward it hand in hand, Reece nodded, remembering the day several months ago when he'd taken Eli to the Geosciences Museum at Virginia Tech. He'd been so captivated by a rock tumbler kit that Reece bought it, then spent the remainder of the weekend trying to ignore the repetitious *klunk-ker-klunk* as the boy polished every last one. It hurt a little when Eli announced that he intended to give the collection to Taylor . . . until he tucked the biggest, shiniest chunk of granite under Reece's pillow. "Now every time you touch it, you can think of me!" The kid sure had a talent for testing a man's ability to keep a lid on his emotions!

"Does your foot hurt more than usual today, Uncle Reece?"

"Nah, probably just a pebble in my shoe."

"Or a wrinkle in your sock. I hate it when that happens."

Most days, his condition — Amniotic

Band Syndrome — was barely detectible. ABS had cut off the blood supply to the big toe of his right foot, effectively amputating it even before he was born. Days when he was on his feet for hours, standing at the operating table or taking a walking tour, like he had today, put extra demands on the remaining toes, his instep, and his sole.

"Yeah," he agreed, "I hate that, too."

"Maybe there's a bench in the gift shop, and you can sit on it to fix your sock."

"Maybe," Reece said, grinning as he opened the gift shop door.

Once inside, Eli turned his jeans pockets inside out and produced two quarters, three pennies, and a dime. "Think this is enough to buy something for Taylor's birthday?" he asked, blowing a denim string from his palm.

"No doubt about it, but are you sure you want to spend *all* of it in one place?"

"Oh, this isn't all of it," he announced, patting his back pocket. "I have some paper money, right here. And if that's still not enough, I have what's in my duck bank."

He'd bought it during their very first nephew-uncle weekend, and once Eli had chosen a spot for it on the bookshelf in his room, Reece dropped in a handful of coins.

"A-a-a-and," he said, "if that's *still* not

enough, I have a whole bunch-a more paper money in my pig bank at home."

"Wow. Where'd you get all that cash!" It felt good, knowing he'd started the boy on a money-saving path.

"Earned it."

The way he said it reminded Reece of the way Taylor had said "of course" when he'd asked if the lemonade was fresh-squeezed.

"No kiddin'? By doing what?"

"Well," he said, counting on pudgy fingers, "by keeping my room neat, and helping Taylor load the dishwasher, and sweeping the front walk, and watering plants . . . stuff like that."

"Important stuff."

"That's what Taylor says." Eli pointed. "Hey, look over there. Jewelry. She *loves* jewelry!"

From the mouths of babes, Reece thought, cringing when he remembered laughing when Dixie compared Taylor to a gypsy. But the guilt was quickly supplanted by pity: if it still hurt this much to think about that loveless relationship, how much more painful were Taylor's memories?

"Can I help you with something, sir?" Bold red letters on her name tag identified her as GLADYS.

He stepped up to the counter. "As a matter of fact, you can." He nodded toward Eli, who was busy spinning an earrings display rack. "My boy has a few dollars in his pocket, but I'm sure it won't be enough to pay for his mom's birthday gift." Peeling two twenties from his money clip, Reece added "If there's any change left over, I want you to keep it, for helping me bolster his ego."

"Oh, I couldn't possibly take your money. I have a grandson about his age, and —"

"But Gladys, if he sees you handing me change, he'll know he's been duped."

She looked at Eli and nodded. "Oh. Yes. I suppose you're right." And then she snickered. "But what if what he buys is *more* than forty dollars?"

He scanned a few of the price tags inside the display cabinet that separated them and saw just how possible that was. "Then you'll have to distract him while I count out the rest." Sliding the silver money clip back into his pocket, he winked. "Thanks, Gladys."

"Thanks for what?" Eli wanted to know. "Did you buy something, too?"

"No. Not yet."

He plunked all of his money onto the counter and pointed at the turquoise set inside the case. "How much for those?"

Gladys turned over the tiny white tag and

announced a price two cents less than what he'd put down.

"Including the little box?"

"Why, of course."

Eli fist-pumped the air. Then his smile faded as he looked up at Reece. "Do you think she'd like it?"

"Y'know, I think she'll love it." He winked at Gladys and said, "We'll take it."

Eli stood on tiptoe, watching as Gladys removed the price tag and placed the set onto a bed of cotton. "If you have a green ribbon, that would be really cool, because green is her favorite color."

Gladys chuckled. "Is that so?"

"Yup. 'Cause my eyes are green." Shoulders hunched, he giggled. "Girls sure have silly reasons to pick favorite stuff."

"Yes, we sure do," Gladys agreed, and snipped off a length of green ribbon. She peered over the black-and-white polka dot frames of her powerful magnifying lenses. "While I'm finishing up here, why don't you see if you can find a pretty card to go with this lovely present. They're on the rack over there by the door. All handmade and mostly blank inside, so you write whatever your heart desires!"

The instant he was out of earshot, Gladys leaned across the counter. "My, my, my.

121

Your boy has expensive taste," she whispered, sliding the tag closer.

His boy. Reece would never get tired of hearing that. He picked it up and read the minuscule numerals. "$375.98? You're kidding, right?"

"I'll have you know that set is crafted from .925 silver and set with genuine turquoise stones. A local artisan makes one-of-a-kind sets, so your wife will never run into anyone wearing anything like it."

His wife? Weird. He liked the sound of that almost as much as he'd liked hearing "his boy." He could blame his peculiar reaction on that whack he'd taken to the side of his head, looking for the source of a leak under the kitchen sink that morning. But how was he to explain how addle-brained he'd felt, sitting at Taylor's kitchen table yesterday?

She wore jewelry like this all the time. Surely it wouldn't take long for her to figure out that Eli couldn't possibly have paid for the set on his own.

He'd barely signed his name to the credit card receipt when Eli returned. "Didn't see anything I liked," he grumped.

"That's okay. You can make her a card," Reece said. "She'll like that better anyway."

That put the smile back onto his face. And

when Gladys handed him the pretty package, the smile grew wider. "So how much is it?" he asked, tapping the coins he'd laid out earlier.

Gladys slid them into her upturned palm, leaving one nickel and a penny behind. "There we go," she said, dropping them into the cash drawer. "Thank you so much for your patronage, sir. Have a nice day!" And with that, she turned to the next customer in line.

"What's patronage?" Eli asked as they crossed the parking lot.

"It means she knows a good customer when she sees one."

"Oh," Eli said. Then "Women sure are expensive, aren't they?"

"Don't I know it," Reece said, laughing. "Don't I know it!"

7

All the way from Reece's townhouse to the Misty Wolf, Eli held the paperback-sized pink box in his lap. *The way he's hanging on to it, you'd think he was carrying a couple ounces of nitroglycerine,* Reece thought, grinning into the rearview mirror. Something told him the boy would have been just as protective if the windows had been up the whole way home.

The instant he parked in his usual spot under the big oak that shaded her circular driveway, Eli unfastened his booster seat and climbed out of the car. "Meet you inside!" he yelled, running toward the house.

Reece chuckled as he followed in tiny footsteps. Even from out here, he could hear Eli, racing from room to room, calling Taylor's name. When he stepped into the foyer a minute later, the excited chant told him that Eli still hadn't found her. It was the very first time she hadn't greeted them at the door. If he was disappointed about that, how must Eli feel?

As he hung the boy's backpack from the newel post, as Taylor always did, Reece blamed her absence on Jimmy Jacobs. Mr. I'm-A-Famous-Singing-Sensation must have made a special request, and Taylor was trying her best to meet it. He put the now-empty cooler beside the sewing basket, which looked just as full now as it had on Friday night. And no wonder, with a trip into town *and* a demanding guest to pamper.

"*There* you are," he heard Eli say. "I've been looking and looking for you everywhere!"

Her merry laughter echoed in the kitchen. "Sorry. I was in the basement, fetching light bulbs."

"I thought we kept those in the hall closet."

"We do now. But when Gran and Gramps owned this place, they stored just about everything down there. And the ones I needed were for that big chandelier in the front hall." She glanced at the clock above the sink. "You guys are right on time, as usual."

Reece could see that it was all Eli could

125

do to keep his eagerness in check. "And bearing gifts," he said, pointing.

Taylor stood on her tiptoes to look over Eli's head. "What's that you're hiding behind your back, young man?"

"It's your birthday present," he said, holding it out.

Her hands were trembling — and so was her lower lip — when she accepted it. "You little sweetheart, you!" she said, kissing his temple. "But my birthday isn't until next week."

"I know, but you don't have to wait until next week. You can open it now if you want to. You want to, right?"

"Are you kidding! Of course I want to!" she said, mussing his hair. "But I'm so excited that my knees are shaking like crazy. How about if we all go into the parlor, so I can sit. I'd hate to *fall* down before I even untie that pretty bow."

A minute later, with Eli seated to her left and Reece on her right, Jimmy walked into the room, grinning like the Cheshire cat . . . until he saw Reece. "Hey," he said, sitting in one of the wingbacks that flanked the fireplace.

"Hey, yourself."

"Taylor is about to open the birthday present I got her," Eli told Jimmy.

"But isn't your birthday next week?"

It galled Reece that Jimmy knew the date, and he didn't.

Taylor, thankfully, ignored the comment. "It's almost too pretty to unwrap," she said, carefully sliding the satiny ribbon aside. "Pink and green, two of my most favorite colors." She handed the bow to Eli, gave the box top to Reece, and peeked under the cotton blanket that covered her present.

A tiny gasp escaped her lips as she held the necklace up to the light. Her voice — somewhere between a whisper and a sigh — wavered when she said, "Oh, Eli. It's . . . it's so *beauti*ful!"

It was worth every penny he'd plunked down to see the look of stunned disbelief on Jimmy Jacobs's face; clearly, the man understood that Eli hadn't paid for the set all by himself. But it would have been worth *five times* what he'd paid to see Taylor's reaction.

When she'd introduced him to the whole "visiting weekends" situation, he'd resented the intrusion into his "I'm in charge" world. Funny what an impact eleven short months could have on a guy's outlook, because now, he planned his whole *life* around those weekends! Taylor had given him that gift, so if a box of overpriced trinkets could bring her this much joy . . . well, who could put a price on that?

Eli crawled over into Reece's lap and put his arm around his neck, and from the corner of his mouth said, "I thought she liked it."

He slid his arm around the boy. "She does," he whispered back. "I'm sure of it."

"Yeah? Then why is she *cryin'*?"

"Because," Taylor answered, "girls are weird. We cry when we're happy, and we cry when we're sad."

Jimmy added "*And* when they're mad."

"Or afraid," Reece put in.

"Oh, brother." Eli groaned and flopped off Reece's lap against the sofa's pillow-back cushions. "Guess that means when I grow up, I'm gonna be just like you, Jimmy."

"Like me?" Jimmy chuckled. "What's *that* mean?"

"A . . . um. . . ." He scratched his head. "What do you call it when a man never gets married?"

"A confirmed bachelor?" Taylor said.

Eli nodded. "Yeah. That's it." He shook his head. " 'Cause I don't think I'll ever, *ever* understand girls."

If that was the prerequisite, Reece thought, the human race would cease to exist. Fortunately, four-year-old boys don't hold on to emotions — especially negative ones — for very long.

"So, are you gonna put it on or not?"

"Of course!" She made a few attempts at fastening the clasp, then groaned. "My hands are shaking too much to do it. But that's okay. A T-shirt and jeans isn't exactly the proper attire for —"

The look of disappointment on Eli's face was enough to prompt Reece to get up. "Here," he said, taking the necklace from her. "Let me help."

Once she was on her feet, he stood behind her, praying as his thumbnail slid back the minuscule silver clasp that Jimmy wouldn't see how badly his own hands were shaking. He dropped the pendant over her head. Over her gorgeous, shining, sweet-smelling blond curls. *Snap out of it, you idiot, because you have an audience.*

He didn't realize he'd been holding his breath until the tiny clasp grabbed the last tiny link. "There," he said, exhaling a sigh of relief, "you are now properly necklaced."

Taylor turned slowly, one hand covering the turquoise pendant, the other fluttering near her throat. "Thank you, thank you so much."

Reece read the silent message transmitted straight to his heart by way of those enormous gray eyes: she was thanking him for helping Eli give her the gift, too. His ears felt hot and his palms went damp. If he didn't get a grip, fast, that smirking cowboy would see him blush like a schoolgirl.

"I, ah, when we came in, I put your cooler beside your sewing basket. The Tay-ghetti was great, by the way. He talked me into warming it up for breakfast."

"Breakfast! Oh, my goodness." And laughing, she added, "I'm happy to hear you guys enjoyed it."

"Speaking of the sewing basket, did you find any time for your project this weekend?"

"What project?" Jimmy wanted to know.

Taylor's mouth slanted in a wry grin. "Oh, it's nothing," she said, pointing at Eli. Facing Reece again, she continued with "No actual *sewing*, I'm afraid, but I did get a lot of the prep work out of the way, thanks to my shopping spree in town yesterday. And now that I have all the supplies I'll need, things should pick up speed. . . ."

She let her voice trail off, and he got the message, loud and clear: the project was a surprise *and* a secret. Something for Eli . . . or for *Jimmy*, he wondered. The question kindled the same smoldering resentment he'd carried after Dixie walked out on him.

130

He told himself that jealousy shouldn't play any role in his relationship with Taylor. For a while, he'd done a fair-to-middlin' job of pretending her merry laughter and rosy outlook didn't drive him crazy. But then Eliot was killed, and Margo died, and his parents continued to put church folk ahead of flesh-and-blood kin. What a sorry state of affairs for poor Eli, Reece used to tell himself, with only the likes of *him* to call family. And then Taylor reminded him by way of her every-other-weekend plan that Eli had more than that . . . and so did *he*. So if this long-haired, tattooed crooner thought he could muscle his way in where he didn't belong, for no reason other than a so-called friendship with Eliot, well, he had another think coming!

When he'd walked into the house earlier, Reece had pretty much decided to put off their scheduling talk for one night this week. But now? After seeing that territorial look on Jimmy's face, Reece wished there was a legitimate reason for *him* to rent a room at the Misty Wolf, too.

8

After Eli's bath, Taylor dressed him in his favorite pajamas. While Taylor puttered in the kitchen, Eli peppered Jimmy with questions about his assortment of guitars. Reece plastered a smile on his face and did his best not to yawn as the guy explained the difference between nylon and steel strings.

"Will you sing me that song," Eli said, "about the lost kids?"

" 'Poor Babes in the Woods'? You bet!"

He picked up his Ovation and rested it on one thigh, and Eli — God love him — huddled up beside Reece.

Jimmy tucked a triangular pick between the tuning strings. "See, this is one of those tunes that sounds better if I use my fingers," he said, producing a soft, full-bodied chord.

Reece had heard him sing before — just about every time he flicked on the car stereo. Much as he hated to admit it, the guy was good. Up-tempo or ballad, poignant or droll, his albums consistently climbed to the top of the charts. It would have been easy, giving credit for his popularity to savvy PR agents, his gifted band, or the skilled engineers in the sound booth, but hearing him live made Reece admit that a blend of raw talent and charisma rather than producer-tweaked studio recordings, explained Jimmy's success.

The irony wasn't lost on Reece when Taylor returned to the living room just as he started an equally sad song, this time about disappointment. Funny how things turn out, Reece thought, because except for wishing he'd been a better son, a more loving brother while he'd had the chance, he had very few regrets. His life was full, his work rewarding, little Eli happy and well-adjusted.

But if that was true, what explained the disquieting awareness that had settled over him lately, hinting that something was missing, something that not even the most extravagant material possessions had the power to lift?

Then Taylor took Eli's face in her hands and got him giggling with Eskimo kisses. Watching the two of them — Taylor, mostly — gave Reece his answer: he had everything a man could want, except for being on the receiving end of love like that.

Suddenly, Taylor stood. "Put that git-fiddle away, Jimmy," she said. "You almost made me forget about the sorbet I dipped up before I came in here." She clapped her hands. "Into the kitchen, boys, before it turns it a soupy, syrupy mess."

If she realized how much control she had over two grown men and the impulsive boy who instantly followed her, like fuzzy ducklings behind their mama, it didn't show. And there, Reece admitted, was the difference between Taylor and women like Dixie.

An easy ambiance filled the room, and even with Jimmy over there, laughing at his own jokes and talking way too loud, Reece felt very much at home.

Eli carried his bowl and spoon to the sink, then climbed into Taylor's lap. Knuckling one eye, he yawned. "Is it okay if Reece tucks me into bed?"

If the request surprised her, that didn't show either. "Of course, it's okay," she said matter-of-factly.

So Reece got to his feet, scooped Eli into his arms, and headed for the back stairs.

"He's really sleepy," she said, fingers around an imaginary toothbrush, "so don't let him forget."

Nodding, he carried Eli to the second

floor. It wasn't until he reached the landing that he realized he'd never been up here before. "Where's your room?" he asked.

And Eli showed him. "Taylor and I share this bathroom. It's called a Jack and Jill," he said, pointing, "because this door leads to her room, and that one leads to mine." Giggling behind one hand, he added, "I wonder what goofy guy named it *that.*"

Reece glanced around the room. She'd done a bang-up job of keeping the place ruffles-and-lace free. The thick, fuzzy rugs scattered across tiny hexagonal black and white tiles matched the pale blue walls, and somehow, she'd found a shade of white that exactly matched the porcelain fixtures. Two toothbrushes hung in the ceramic rack beneath the mirrored medicine cabinet. "Is this one is yours?" he asked, pointing at the pink one.

"No way! Pink is for *girls!*" He stepped up onto a stool that said NOW ELI IS BIG ENOUGH! and grabbed the one with the Spiderman handle, and squeezed a dollop of blue gel onto its bristles. He spent all of a minute, scrubbing his teeth before rinsing the brush.

"Whoa there," Reece said, turning off the water. "We've got to do a better job than that, or —"

"I know, I know," Eli moaned, "or I'll end up looking like *that.*"

He tapped the tennis ball, stuffed into the mouth of a red Solo cup. Taylor, Reece guessed, had drawn eyes and a nose, and made the two-inch slit that served as its mouth.

Eli plucked it from the cup, and squeezing it, made the mouth open and close. "If you don't brush and floss," he said in a falsetto voice, "you'll end up toothless and mis'rable, just like me." He put the ball back where he'd found it and snickered. "Don't look at me . . . that was Taylor's idea."

"Well, she's right, you know," he said, trying not to chuckle. Leave it to her to come up with a nonbossy way to teach the boy about proper oral hygiene.

"I know," Eli droned. Then he reloaded the brush, and this time, did the job properly. "After I say my prayers, will you read me *Alexander*?" he asked, voice muffled by the hand towel.

"Sure." One of these days, he'd get the hang of this bedtime prayers thing. Until then, he did his best to mask resentment against the parents who'd always been more interested in teaching village children to pray than their own. If that was an example of Christian love, they could —

"Dear God," Eli began, "it's me again, Eli Reece Bradley. From Blacksburg, Virginia, remember? I know it's a little later than usual, but Jimmy was singing and Taylor made pineapple sorbet, and nobody can pass up a bowl of *that* stuff. So anyway, if my mom and dad are close by, please tell them I miss them very, very much. Especially Mom. But only 'cause I knew her longer. And better. On account-a Dad was away a lot, being a soldier."

He opened one eye and whispered to Reece "Wouldn't want to hurt Dad's feelings, y'know?"

"No, you wouldn't want to do that." Mentally, he added another item to his "Reasons to Dislike Eliot" list: if the fool hadn't always put his precious Marines ahead of everything and everyone else. . . .

"Thank you for my house and my toys and always having plenty of food to eat. God bless my horses — Millie and Alvin and Bert and Elsie. Bless Isaac and Tootie, and my teacher, Mrs. Cunningham, and my best-best friend Randy." He paused. "If you get a minute, maybe you could maybe fix Randy's legs, 'cause he'd really, *really* like to play Little League with the rest of us." He gave a little nod, as if to confirm the request, before continuing. "God bless

Jimmy and Taylor and my second-best friend, Uncle Reece. Amen."

He scrambled into bed, then tossed back the covers and hung his legs over the side. "All set," he said, handing Reece the storybook.

Laughing to himself, Reece turned to the first page and read, " 'It was bedtime. Chris and his father sat side by side on Chris's bed —' "

"Just like we're doing!"

"Yep."

He looked into Reece's face. "Do you think if my dad wasn't in heaven, he'd read me stories, like you and Taylor do?"

" 'Course he would. And so would your mom."

"Maybe."

Maybe? Though Reece didn't understand, he read a few more pages, stopping when Eli ran his fingertip across a crayon scrawl. "Taylor did that when she was a little girl. Did you know this used to be her book?"

"No, I sure didn't." But it made sense, given the tattered and frayed binding.

"She gave it to me when I turned four, and told me I have to take extra special very good care of it, because her dad gave it to her when *she* turned four."

The image of Taylor — blonde braids

bouncing as she skipped through life — flashed in his mind.

"Did you know *her* father died when she was little, too?"

"Yeah, I did," he said, though he didn't know many of the details.

"Wonder if Randy got his new leg braces today. He got too big for the old ones, you know."

Reece nodded. As Randy's doctor, he'd been the one to suggest a larger pair.

Eli doubled up his little fists, brought them down on the mattress. "What *is* that sickness he has, anyway?"

Reece closed the book and slid an arm across the boy's shoulders. "Well, something happened to Randy's brain, even before he was born, something that messed up his leg muscles." He had two other patients born with Muscular Dystrophy, but unlike Randy — who could walk and talk and do most of the things his friends could do — both of them were confined to wheelchairs. It's where Randy would end up eventually, but for now . . .

"Why did God do it to him? I mean, Randy's a good kid."

Eli fixed his gaze on Reece's face and waited for a straight answer to what he thought was a simple question. Reece understood the boy's doubts because just over a year ago — moments after Margo's coffin was lowered into the ground — he'd asked a similar question himself. The preacher's graveside mumbo-jumbo had only raised more questions. Did the preacher — did *God* — really expect him to hold onto faith in the face of back-to-back heartache? If a full-grown man couldn't make sense of it, how could he explain it to this bighearted, innocent kid who'd lost both parents in the course of a year!

If You're listening, Lord, I sure could use a little direction, here.

He pulled Eli onto his lap. "I think . . . I think maybe God chose Randy to teach people things."

Eli harrumphed. "He's *four,* Uncle Reece. That's not old enough to teach anybody anything."

"Oh, that's where you're wrong, kiddo." Lifting the boy's chin on a bent forefinger, he said, "Randy is plenty old enough to teach us things. By watching him, we learn how much we can accomplish if we work hard, if we don't whine and complain, if we refuse to quit. Randy wears braces on his legs, but he does his best to keep up with you and the rest of the kids at school, doesn't he?"

Eli nodded.

"And he has a hard time holding pencils and crayons, but that didn't stop him from helping his mom fill out all those invitations to his birthday party, did it?"

"No, but. . . ." Frowning, Eli shook his head. "But wouldn't it be easier for God to just *put* that kind of stuff into everybody's head on the day we're born?"

Hate to be a pest, Lord, but the kid's got a point. . . . Then he spotted Eli's high-topped sneakers on the shelf in his closet. And right beside them, the Velcro-tabbed pair he'd worn before he learned to tie his shoes. "How did you learn to tie your shoes?"

Eli shrugged. "Taylor showed me."

"And those first couple of times, you felt like a big fumble-fingers, didn't you?"

"*I'll* say."

"But if she came to your rescue every time you failed, do you think you would have ever learned how to do it, all by yourself?"

He tucked in one corner of his mouth. "No, I guess not." He met Reece's gaze to add, "But that still doesn't make things easier for Randy."

"No, I guess not," he echoed, kissing the top of Eli's head. "But that's okay, because all Randy needs from you is to know that you're his friend, and that you'll help him

141

any time he needs it."

Eli snuggled up and closed the book. "Maybe Taylor will let me bring *Alexander* in my backpack next time I go to your house." Yawning, he climbed under the covers and stretched. "And that can be one of my bedtime stories, since we didn't finish it tonight."

Reece put the book back on the shelf and turned out the light. And by the time he turned around, Eli was fast asleep. "I sure do love you, little buddy," he whispered, pressing a gentle kiss to the boy's forehead. He was halfway out the door when Eli rolled onto his side. "I love you, too, Uncle Reece."

Reece's shoes seemed nailed to the floor as he hung his head and prayed for the strength to fight off the tears, stinging his eyes. "Lord, make me into a better man," he whispered, "the kind of man Eli deserves as a dad."

9

Tootie stood frowning at Taylor's kitchen calendar. "How can it be June already?" she asked, biting the point off a carrot.

Isaac dropped a kiss onto her cheek on his way to the sink. "Guess it's true what they say . . ."

The hiss of water, spewing from the faucet to the sudsy dishwater, nearly drowned out her quiet question. "What do they say?"

"That time flies when you're having fun."

"Hmpf. If that's the case, these big black letters should say January, not June."

"Is that your way of saying your life's no fun?"

"No." She frowned. "Not exactly."

"My advice to you is . . . try and be a little more like me; do your best to *make* every day fun."

Tootie planted both fists on her hips and did her best to look annoyed. "Easy for you to say. You're not on the receiving end of your . . . fun."

His mug disappeared into the suds. "You can fool some guys some of the time," he said as his spoon joined it, "but you can't fool me." Turning, he added "I remember the way you used to be . . . before . . . you know."

"No. I don't know, but I'm sure you'll enlighten me." She crossed both arms over her chest. "Before what?"

Tootie's eyes widened as he scooped up a palm full of bubbles. "Don't even think about it, mister," she said as he walked toward her, "or I'll —"

He slid his free hand behind her waist and pulled her into a hug. "Or you'll *what?*"

Taylor stifled a groan. Most days, their wordplay and tom-foolery was as much fun as a Tracy-Hepburn movie.

Today wasn't one of those days.

The Misty Wolf had been booked to capacity every day for the past two months . . . a good thing, since Tootie and Isaac depended on the inn's revenue almost as much as Taylor did. But success like that came at a price: long days, hard work, and a dizzying schedule. Taylor considered herself lucky if she clocked more than four hours' sleep in a row.

She blamed her fast-growing list of "if

144

onlys . . ."

If only she could afford to hire someone to clean the Misty Wolf.

If only she could stop worrying about the Jimmy-has-a-crush-on-you nonsense Tootie had planted in her head.

If only she'd stop wondering why Reece's behavior toward her had gone from almost warm to nearly as standoffish as when they'd met.

If only Tootie and Isaac worked as much as they bickered.

"If you two don't stop your squabbling, you'll drive me crazy!"

In the silence that followed, her grand-father's favorite quote echoed in her mind: *"If," biggest li'l word in the English language.* If she'd known the little word had the power to end their back-and-forth teasing, she'd have used it long ago.

But she had no desire to hurt their feelings. "I seem to recall the two of you promising to help me come up with some ideas for Eli's birthday party," she said, forcing a grin.

"It's hard to think on an empty stomach."

Tootie gasped. "Why, Isaac Williams, it hasn't even been an hour since you wolfed down that bacon-and-eggs breakfast I made you. You can't *possibly* be hungry already!"

"I'm like an old coal furnace," he said, grinning and patting his flat belly. "You gotta feed this baby real good to keep it going."

"I'm beginning to believe you really *do* have a hollow leg, because in all the time I've known you, I don't think I've ever heard you say you're full!"

Taylor might as well have been talking to that sink full of dirty dishes for all the good her complaint had done. Could it be that she'd been such a grump lately that her flare-up only seemed out of character to *her*?

"I need to run a few errands," she said, grabbing her purse from the hook behind the door. She didn't write up the customary list of chores to keep them busy while she was gone. Didn't say good-bye. Didn't tell them where she was going or when she'd be home, mostly because she didn't know if she'd head for Blacksburg or Christiansburg or across the Parrott River. The one thing Taylor knew for sure was that if she didn't put some distance between herself and them, she'd end up apologizing for saying something mean-spirited.

The screen door hadn't even closed yet before Tootie said, "What's she thinking, taking off without a word? The place is full-

146

up; what if one of the guests needs —"

"Now, now . . . there's not a young'un among 'em, and they all know that they're on their own for supper."

"But what if they ask for a map or a restaurant recommendation or directions to —"

"We've both been around here long enough to answer any questions they might have."

Taylor heard Tootie's exasperated sigh.

"I suppose you're right. But still, it isn't like Taylor to just up and leave that way."

"You said yourself, just yesterday, that she's been acting a little hinky these past few days. Maybe a couple hours, off on her own, is just what the doctor ordered."

"I always wondered when it would all get to be too much for her."

Taylor could picture Tootie, aiming that maternal pointer finger at Isaac as she spoke.

"With all these guests, and the horses, and Eli. . . ."

"Calm down," Isaac said. "We don't need *two* hysterical females around here."

Hysterical? Is *that* the way they saw her now? Taylor stopped walking so suddenly that she nearly lost her balance.

"She'll pull herself together, just like she

has every other time something freaked her out."

She could have hugged Isaac for saying that. But . . . every other time? *When have I ever freaked out!*

"Remember when the tornadoes peeled every shingle off the barn roof? And that time that hippy rock band booked the place and tore up all the bathrooms? She held it together when Eliot died overseas, and you know as well as I do that if it hadn't been for Taylor's clearheadedness, Margo would have killed herself with pills *long* before she crashed her car into that tree. Taylor's barely bigger than a minute, but she's got the constitution of a bull moose."

Taylor slumped against the railing and made a mental note to find a proper way to thank Isaac for his support.

"Don't know about you," he continued, "but I aim to pull a little more of the weight around here while she's under the gun."

"You're right. I'll help out more, too." Tootie hesitated before saying "I just wish I knew what was eating at her this time."

This time? *To hear Tootie tell it, a person would think I fly off the handle on a daily basis!*

"Just between you and me, I'd say her problem is heart-related."

That inspired a chuckle from Tootie.

"Heart-related!" she echoed. "What are you talking about, you silly man, you?"

"Taylor doesn't know it yet, but she's in love."

Love? *Me?* Even if she could spare the time — and she most certainly could *not* — Taylor didn't have the patience for anything so frivolous as romance. Besides, *if* she was in love, wouldn't *she* know it as well as she knew that the Misty Wolf was her favorite place in all the world? It took every ounce of her self-control to keep from shouting, *Isaac Williams, you're out of your ever-lovin' mind!*

"I know one person who'll be only too happy to hear that."

Nothing could have surprised Taylor more than to hear Tootie add "Jimmy."

Taylor stifled a gasp as Isaac said, "No, *not* Jimmy."

"Surely you don't mean that fuddy-duddy uncle of Eli's."

Taylor sagged to the bottom step and held her head in her hands. Had she really allowed herself to grow so weak and self-centered that a few nights without sleep could make her act like a spoiled brat? A brat who worried her friends to the point of making wild guesses to explain her horrible behavior? Because seriously . . . in love?

With Reece Montgomery? Ridiculous!

She'd never convince them of that with words. The only way to prove that her feelings for Reece were strictly platonic was to show them.

Starting now.

The screen door squealed so loudly when she went back inside that Taylor cringed. *Should've oiled that hinge last week when you first noticed the squeak,* she thought, hanging her purse behind the door. Between Little Orphan Annie and Scarlet O'Hara, she had plenty of role models to lead her into tomorrow.

Grabbing her apron, she gave it a good flap and plastered a smile on her face. What better way to make up for her mini-tantrum than by getting an early start on their favorite meal: oven-fried chicken and all the fixins. "So listen, you guys," she asked tying the apron behind her waist, "what do you think about combining Eli's birthday party with our annual July 4th cookout?"

Isaac's expression remained skeptical, but he nodded. "Sounds like a good idea to me."

Tootie stepped up beside him. "You were smart, keeping things low-key the way you did last year, when the poor little thing had only been with you a few weeks." She shrugged. "But now? Why, he feels so much at home here that nobody would ever guess he hasn't lived here his entire life. If that doesn't call for a cake, fireworks, *and* a parade, I don't know what does!"

She'd done her best to make him feel that everything she owned was his, too, but the real credit for his rapid adjustment went to Eli himself . . . and the fact that kids were far more resilient than adults. Easygoing and quick to accept the hand he'd been dealt made her all the more determined to get back to work on his quilt, before his life with Eliot and Margo faded so deep into his past that he couldn't summon them to memory.

Taylor sprayed cooking oil into a baking pan. "We'll decorate the whole house with streamers and banners and flags." After tearing off a sheet of waxed paper, she laid it on the counter and covered it with saltines. "I'll even whip up a cake that's red, white, and blue," she said as her rolling pin turned them into crumbs.

Standing at the calendar again, Tootie counted the weeks. "We don't have much time to get invitations into the mail," she said, tapping the July page.

But Isaac waved away her concerns. "Aw, quit your worrying, woman. Three weeks is plenty of time. It isn't like we've got White

House dignitaries and movie stars on the guest list."

Tootie held up a forefinger, as if testing wind direction. "Speaking of stars," she said, "what's *Jimmy* doing over the 4th?"

Taylor cracked two eggs into a wide-mouthed bowl and proceeded to fork-beat them into yellow froth. "I'm not sure." Not an outright fib, but not exactly the truth either. "I'll get online later and check his tour schedule."

"Why don't you just call him instead?"

Taylor gritted her teeth.

"I'm only asking because if he isn't on the road, you *know* that Eli would want him here."

Tootie was right, of course. But admitting it would only open the door to more Jimmy's-in-love-with-you remarks.

"He sent me his itinerary in an e-mail a couple weeks back," Isaac said. "When I get back to my quarters, I can check . . . if you want me to."

"Listen to him," Tootie said, giggling. " 'Back to my quarters.' The way he says it, folks might think he lives in a fancy suite at the Waldorf!"

While they started up a whole new verbal sparring match, Taylor remembered how Isaac's modest accommodations became his permanent home.

Within a week of inheriting Misty Acres from the grandparents who'd raised her, Taylor realized she needed help taking care of the house and surrounding acres. Her ad in the local paper brought twelve strapping men to the door, each with impressive endorsements from former employers. And then Isaac showed up in his rumpled camo shirt, faded jeans, and sporting a diamond stud in his left earlobe and a long gray ponytail. "Never worked as an overseer before," he admitted as she read his résumé, "but I'm a quick study and I'm not afraid of hard work." She'd hired him on the spot, and that very afternoon, they turned the solidly built two-room out-building into his living quarters.

"What're you smiling about?" he asked, breaking into her thoughts.

"Oh, nothing. But the better question is . . . what's on *your* mind?"

Turning toward Tootie, he pretended to hide his pointer finger behind a cupped hand. "Can't get anything past this one," he said in a loud whisper. And facing Taylor, he added "To answer your question, I was just wondering when you last took a good long look at Millie?"

She moved a chicken thigh from the egg

mixture to the cracker crumbs, and dropped it into the baking pan. "This morning," she said, "when I fed and watered her." She grabbed a drumstick, and gave it the same treatment. "Why?"

"Did she seem . . ." He frowned. "I don't know, a little 'off' to you?"

Come to think of it, the mare had been a bit lethargic lately. Until now, she'd blamed it on the unpredictable weather — hot and sunny one day, raw and rainy the next — that kept Millie in her stall instead of outside, running free in the paddock.

Isaac helped himself to a cracker. "Maybe all she needs," he said, crunching, "is some TLC. Soon as I finish this snack, I'll brush her 'til her coat gleams!"

Tootie harrumphed. "You'd best take care, or the poor filly will end up bald."

"She hasn't been a filly for close to six months now."

Tootie's shoulders sagged. "I know, I know," she droned, "fillies are four years old or less, and —"

"It's good to hear that you pay attention to *some* of the things I say." He faced Taylor to add, "But Tootie makes a good point. Too much brushing will irritate her skin. You know how sensitive that horse is. So if that isn't what's eating her, what *is*?"

"How about a good rub-down instead? She likes that every bit as much as being brushed."

Unfortunately, work on the quilt would just have to wait — again — until Eli and the *Misty Wolf* guests had settled in for the night. Snipping and stitching always had a calming effect on her; maybe tonight it will relax her enough to catch *five* hours' sleep instead of three or four.

Taylor slid the tray of cracker-coated chicken into the oven and set the timer for ninety minutes, and taking the back stairs two at a time, dashed into her room to trade her flip-flops for work boots. On the way through the kitchen, she grabbed a few raw carrots from the fridge, then jogged toward the barn.

"How about some music, girl?" she asked, turning on the CD player. Millie loved the old classics, and as a Tchaikovsky sonata began to waft from the dual speakers, she remembered an article she'd read, months ago. "Just be thankful that we don't live in England," she said, finger-combing the mare's dark gray forelock. "Remember that story about the poor woman who was fined for playing the radio for her horses?"

Ears pricked forward, Millie bobbed her head.

"How crazy and unfair was *that*?"

She slipped the curry comb onto her hand and began brushing. Each slow, gentle stroke increased the gloss of the gray-speckled hair. Millie nickered quietly — a sure sign that she was enjoying the attention. "Since you're being such a good girl," Taylor whispered, ruffling her thick, dark mane, "maybe I'll give you some braids and bows."

Millie swished her long glossy tail, and Taylor read it to mean the horse wanted no part of it. Laughing, she hugged her. "We don't have a whole lot in common, but we'll always have that, won't we?"

Taylor had always been a bit of a tomboy. As a girl, chin-length curls guaranteed less time in front of the mirror and more time on horseback, in the treetops, or fishing at the river-bank, and she'd worn the style right into adulthood. Mark loved to tease her, saying "Bet I'm the only guy on the planet whose best girl hates fussing with her hair . . . but won't leave the house without a pair of dangly earrings on." She couldn't very well argue with him, since she didn't understand it herself.

"Ah, well," she said, moving to Millie's other side, "such is life, eh, girl?" The quote reminded her of her grandmother, who could fire off a witty adage to fit almost any situation. "You were just a foal when Gran died, so you never had the pleasure of hearing her silly sayings. Like 'I'm gonna live forever, or die trying!' and 'If you put those two in a sack, no telling which one would crawl out first!' And my favorite, 'God and nature have decreed that I'll age, but I refuse to get old!' "

Smiling, Taylor hummed along with the Allegro Giusto section. The music roused a memory of the first time she'd heard the melody: two days before her seventh birthday, when her mom had taken her to see a dinner theater production of *Swan Lake.*

Two days after *that,* her mom and dad were gone from her life. Forever.

Millie swung her head around and rested her chin on the back of Taylor's hand. "Is that your clever way of telling me I should get back to work, or that you've had enough of this for one afternoon?"

But even as she spoke the words, Taylor knew that wasn't the reason for Millie's affectionate gesture. The horse had always been attuned to her moods, and this was no exception.

"And I love you, too," she whispered.

Taylor returned the brush to its proper place on the shelf and grabbed the hoof

157

pick. "I declare," she said, tucking the horse's right-front hoof between her knees, "if I live to be a hundred, I'll never figure out how your hooves get so full of gunk, even on days when you aren't out riding the trails!"

Millie chose that moment to steal one of the carrots tucked into Taylor's back jeans pocket. "Hey!" she said, laughing. "That was supposed to be your reward for not stomping on my toes."

But the treat was gone, even before Taylor could put the hoof pick back where it belonged. "The way you've been gobbling up everything in sight lately makes a body wonder if you're eating for two." But except for sluggishness and an increased appetite, Millie displayed none of the other signs of pregnancy. Besides, if Taylor *had* a mind to breed Millie, she'd have done it last fall, not only so that she'd have some say in what the foal would look like, but to give the little thing plenty of time to grow healthy and strong before the snows started swirling.

She plucked another carrot from her pocket and held it near Millie's nose. "The chicken will be ready to come out of the oven before we know it, so —"

Her cell phone buzzed from deep in the bib pocket of her coveralls. "Good grief," she muttered, glancing at the caller ID, "it's Jimmy."

Millie munched contentedly as Taylor punched the Talk button. "Hey, you, what's up?"

"Just realized what day it is, and thought I'd give you a call, make sure you're okay."

What day it is? And then it hit her: five years ago today, the doctors diagnosed Mark with Stage 4 pancreatic cancer. She pictured his handsome young face, contorted with shock and confusion as the oncologist handed him an inch-thick stack of brochures, compiled to help patients cope with a terminal diagnosis. But how like Mark to shake off his own fear and grab her hand . . . to comfort *her.* Had she subconsciously pushed the awful date from her mind? It would go a long way in explaining what had put her into this strange funk these past few days.

"Taylor? You still there?"

"Yes, yes I'm here."

"How're you doing?"

"I'm fine." And then it dawned on her that Jimmy — an only child — had known Mark far longer than she had. Over the years, Mark became more his brother than his friend; if memory of this date rattled her, how much had it affected him? "And how 'bout *you?*"

"I'm fine," he echoed.

In her experience, it was always better not to dwell on sadness. "Isaac and Tootie and I are planning Eli's birthday party," she said, forcing a cheeriness into her voice that she didn't feel. "July 4th falls on a Saturday this year, and since that's his actual birth date, we thought it'd be nice to combine the festivities."

"Sounds great. Wish I could be there."

A peculiar mix of disappointment and relief swirled in her heart. "Why can't you be here?"

"Because I'm doing a concert at the Scottrade Center in St. Louis on the 3rd —"

"Oh. That's a shame."

"— nearly 700 miles from my favorite girl."

Taylor held her breath and prayed that God would help her come up with a response that wouldn't hurt his feelings. Or send the wrong message. "Why not get online to look for one of those cheap flights they're advertising, and sneak away, just for the day?" The words were no sooner out of her mouth before she remembered that just last Christmas, he'd bought a 2001 Lear jet.

"I, ah, I guess that might be something to

consider . . ."

". . . if you didn't have a plane of your very own, you mean?" she finished for him. *Take a nap, you big goof, so you'll have the presence of mind to* think *before you talk!*

Millie whinnied and pawed the stall floor.

"Oh. Hey. I didn't realize you were in the barn. Guess I should have asked if I was interrupting anything."

"You aren't. I was spending a little quality time with my best girl, here."

"Give her a pat for me." A pause, and then "So tell me, how's *my* best girl?"

Don't jump to conclusions, harebrain. He's probably talking about Millie. "Oh, just being her old self," she said as the horse grabbed the last carrot. "Stealing carrots, eating and sleeping like there's no tomorrow, stomping around and pouting when she can't get outside to run and play." It was all Taylor could do to choke back a giggle, because how silly would all that sound if Jimmy hadn't been referring to Millie!

"Takes a load off my mind knowing that if the Misty Wolf ever goes under, you can find other work . . . as a comedian." He cleared his throat. "Guess I'd better let you get back to brushin' that old nag. No point giving her another excuse to pout, right?"

"Right." He'd laughed quietly as he said

it, but Taylor didn't know how to explain his suddenly gritty tone. "Thanks for calling. And if you can rearrange your schedule for Eli's party, just say the word. The place is already booked up for that weekend, but someone could cancel. Or you can bunk down in the library."

Jimmy sounded a little more like his jovial self when he said, "Not my first choice, but beggars can't be choosers, can they? Besides, I'd rather sleep on the floor than bunk down at that fleabag motel on 412 again."

After a moment of "take care"s and "see you soon"s, he hung up.

She snapped the phone shut and dropped it into her shirt pocket. "Now really," she said, pressing her forehead to Millie's, "does he expect me *not* to book his favorite suite, 'just in case'?"

The horse bobbed her head.

"Makes y'wonder why Tootie — or anybody else, for that matter — thinks I want to spend the rest of my life linked to a moody musician, doesn't it."

The question reminded her of Isaac's earlier observation that she was falling in love with Reece. "Falling, but unaware of it," she grumbled.

Taylor pictured his mop of dark hair, his bright green eyes. Memory of his slightly crooked grin painted a dreamy smile on her own face, and when she caught herself at it, Taylor loosed a groan of frustration.

"Hard to believe a guy who's big and broad enough to be a quarterback could be afraid of an animal as sweet-tempered as you, isn't it?"

Millie pawed the floor again, then snorted, a subtle reminder that she could be as high-strung as a royal Arabian when she wanted to be. "I suppose you're right. Men — and thoroughbreds — haven't exactly cornered the market on 'temperamental,' have they?"

Taylor filled Millie's feedbag and water trough, and in her hurry to check on the fried chicken, tugged a little too hard on the latch. The stall gate smacked her anklebone hard enough that the *clunk* startled the horse. It reminded her of an afternoon, soon after Eliot and Margo returned from their honeymoon, when she'd asked her new sister-in-law if a football injury had caused Reece's slight limp. But he'd thumped into the room before Margo had a chance to answer . . . and the look on his face was enough to tell Taylor it wasn't a topic they discussed in the Montgomery family.

"I need to be more like you," she said, turning out all but the light above the tool bench, "and convince every one of 'em that

I'm perfectly content and complete without a man in my life." *Maybe if you say that often enough — and with enough conviction — you can convince yourself, too.*

Millie was still bobbing her head as Taylor latched the big double doors.

As she headed up the path, Taylor checked the timer. Eighteen minutes, yet, before the fried chicken needed to come out of the oven. She waved to two of her guests, just returning from a hike near the river. "Having fun?" she hollered.

"You bet!" they hollered back.

They reached the porch at the same time as Taylor.

"Taylor, dear," Peggy said, "that view is simply spectacular. I sure hope the pictures I took turn out."

"They're digital, hon," said her husband. "Only way to ruin them is to hit the camera's delete button."

"You know, I've grown so accustomed to this newfangled gizmo that I nearly forgot about that!"

Laughing, they followed Taylor into the kitchen, where Peggy flopped onto the nearest chair and fanned herself. "Pete, sweetie, get out your checkbook and sit down here. I want to book the same room for this week, next year."

Pete's brow furrowed slightly. "You sure you wouldn't rather come back in the fall, when it's a little cooler?"

"Absolutely not. Now pay this sweet girl. Can't you see she's just itching to get busy with something?"

Taylor grinned. "It only looks that way because I can sense that my timer is about to buzz." Midday meals weren't normally included with the B&B's amenities, but since she'd made enough to feed all of the guests, Tootie and Isaac, and Eli, she decided to make an exception. "I'm serving an impromptu lunch in half an hour," she said, taking salad fixins from the fridge. "Nothing fancy, but you're more than welcome to join us in the dining room."

Peggy slapped a hand onto the table, rattling the salt and pepper shakers and startling Pete enough that he dropped his checkbook. She picked it up and, winking, waved it under his nose. "If you don't pay her, by golly, I will."

Pete sat across from his wife and fished a ballpoint from his fanny pack. "Are you married, Taylor?"

"No." And she saw no reason to tell him more.

"Well, if you ever decide to take the plunge, see to it that you treat your poor husband with a little more deference."

Anyone eavesdropping on the conversation might get the impression that Pete and Peggy weren't overly fond of one another. But Taylor, standing in the glow of their decades-long love, knew better. And for the first time in a long time, her heart ached with longing for the warmth and companionship she'd shared with Mark.

"Fool thing's out of ink," Pete said, shaking his pen. "Peggy? Do you have one that writes?"

While Peggy searched her pouch, Taylor said, "I don't need a deposit right now. I'll pencil you in for this week next year, and send you a reminder in January." She shrugged. "Life's funny; who knows what could come up between now and then?"

Pete got to his feet. "You're a doll, Taylor," he said, extending a hand to his wife.

As Peggy took it, she said, "We'll just freshen up a bit and meet you in the dining room in thirty minutes. And maybe while we're eating, you'll tell me more about that quilt I saw poking out of the sewing basket in the parlor."

"Maybe," Taylor said, tossing the salad. *And maybe not.* So far, Eli had no interest in the contents of the basket, and she intended to keep it that way for as long as possible. "Would you mind rapping on your neighbors' doors to let them know they're welcome to join us, too?"

"Of course," they said together.

The timer buzzed as they disappeared around the corner, and after silencing it, Taylor turned off the oven. The drumsticks and thighs would stay warm and grow even crispier while she set the table and put last night's apple cobbler on the buffet.

The grandfather clock chimed. "Eleven forty-five," she whispered. Time enough to call Reece? He might have to decline if there were patients scheduled, but if not, Eli would love the surprise visit.

And even more surprising, so would she.

10

"I know it's last-minute, but then, so was this crazy idea of mine."

He could almost see her, leaning against the kitchen wall where her clunky old dial phone hung. He'd been avoiding her, partly because he didn't know how much longer he could keep his opinions of her good buddy to himself. According to the TV news, the singer had homes in three European cities, Nashville, and L.A., as well as a tour bus the size of a small ranch house. So why was he spending so much time at the Misty Wolf? It wouldn't have bothered him nearly as much if Eli hadn't picked up so many of Jimmy's mannerisms, and some of the singer's bad habits, too.

"What crazy idea?"

"To serve lunch to my guests. Not that we consider you a guest. Exactly. But if you can make it, I'll set a place for you."

We meaning Taylor and Eli . . . or Taylor

and *Jimmy*?

"Who'll be there?"

"Just the two couples who are staying with us through the weekend," she said, "and Isaac and Tootie."

Good, he thought, no mention of Jimmy. Maybe between now and the time Eli was tucked in for the night, he could figure out a nonthreatening way to broach the touchy subject.

"How soon would you need me there?" Reece did some quick mental math: fifteen, maybe twenty minutes to tie things up here at the office, another ten to drive home and get into jeans and a T-shirt, an additional twenty to drive to her place.

"Oh, this is a very 'come as you are . . . whenever' sort of gathering. It's nothing fancy — just oven-fried chicken and some sides — and like I said, very impromptu. So unless you're a purist."

"A purist?"

"You know, one of those people who prefers his chicken hot? It's fine if you are, because it won't be any trouble at all to nuke a leg or a thigh or whatever when you get here."

Reece chuckled. "I've been a bachelor way too long to be picky about stuff like that." The real truth, in his opinion? The only thing that tasted good straight out of *that* appliance was popcorn. And only then if it was cooked exactly long enough. Given a choice, he'd choose a cold-from-the-fridge drumstick over rubbery microwaved chicken any day. Besides, it'd be great, seeing Eli on an "off" weekend. Especially one that didn't involve Jimmy.

Taylor must have read his silence to mean he was searching for a polite way to say no, because she said, "If you have patients to see or hospital rounds to make . . ."

Her voice trailed off, and then he heard her take a gulp of air.

"Oh my goodness," she whispered. And groaned. "What was I thinking! I can be such a ditz. I should have known you'd have other plans. It's no big deal. Really. I haven't said anything to Eli yet, so there's no chance he'll be disappointed."

Was it his imagination, or did *she* sound disappointed? "As it happens, I'm footloose and fancy-free, as they say. It's just, well, I looked at the appointment book this morning, and would you believe I can't remember if I have more patients to see or not?"

"Oh, I'd believe it all right. And if I had a dollar for every time that's happened to me, I could probably hire that housekeeper I've been dreaming about for years."

When they'd sat side by side at the re-hearsal dinner all those years ago, her nonstop giggling and nervous chatter had been the reason he'd labeled her a dizzy blonde. The gypsylike clothes, bangle brace-lets, and dangly earrings only proved to ce-ment his opinion, and that was *before* long-haired musicians and glassy-eyed artists started frequenting the Misty Wolf. But in the months since Eli had moved in with her, the way she ran the B&B and cared for Eli forced him to reconsider his opinion.

"At the very least," she continued, "I'd have enough for a down payment on a cruise."

Reece chuckled quietly. "How 'bout if I check with Maureen and Gina and get back to you."

"Okay, but you don't need to call first. You're family, and family is always wel-come."

In the span of two minutes, he'd gone from not quite being a guest to family, even now that Eliot and Margo — their main connection — were gone?

The silver-framed photo of Eli, front and center on his big glass-topped desk re-minded him of a bond that would last a lifetime.

"If it turns out I can make it, what can I bring?"

"Nothing . . . except a man-sized appetite. I don't know what got into me. Made enough chicken to feed a small army."

When she punctuated the statement with a merry laugh, his ears went hot and his palms grew damp. He hadn't exactly lived a monk's life, so he didn't understand why he had nothing to compare the feelings to.

"Well," he said, "better get crackin' if I hope to take off early."

Had she said good-bye before hanging up? Had *he*? Reece honestly couldn't remember.

"Somebody put chewing gum on your phone, doc?"

The suddenness of his secretary's voice startled him.

"I was just wondering if maybe that's why it's stuck to the side of your head."

He glanced at the handset. "Oh. Right," he said, and hung up.

Gina's left brow rose slightly on her forehead. "So you're footloose and fancy-free tonight, are you?"

The exact words he'd used, moments ago.

Gina and her mom had been with him for eight years, and in all that time, he'd racked up one complaint: to them, an open door was as good as an engraved invitation to listen in on his calls.

"Like I'm always telling Mom — you live a charmed life."

A charmed life. Right. With parents who preferred life in war-torn countries on other continents to spending time with their own kids, a sister so weak-willed that she'd mourned herself to death, an ex-fiancée who'd left him high and —

He ground his molars together and willed the self-pitying thoughts away. "Any patients left to see this afternoon?" he asked.

"Nope, we're through for the day. So is it okay for Mom and me to duck out early?"

His cell phone buzzed, and recognizing the number, he hit Talk. "Annie, darlin', what can I do for you today?"

And knowing Maureen and Gina would never ask to leave without first dotting every *i* and crossing every *t,* he said, "Have a good weekend."

"Will do," she whispered. "You, too!"

Annie's gravelly voice grated into his ear. "I just thought you should know that pesky cat is back, and this time, it upended *both* of your trash cans."

He winced. "Aw, man . . . how big a mess did she make this time?"

"Not to worry, handsome," Annie said. "I've already taken care of it."

At seventy-three, Annie Landers was the self-appointed guardian of the neighborhood. Nothing got by the woman who seemed determined to walk in her famous namesake's shoes, a fact that had distinct plusses . . . and an equal number of minuses.

"I called Animal Control," she continued. "Oy! What a waste of taxpayers' money. Why, I'd be surprised to find out there's one functioning brain cell among 'em. Do you know what the young fella on the phone said?"

No, Reece did not, but experience told him that if he remained quiet long enough, Annie would tell him.

"Said he'd be happy to deliver a have-a-heart trap . . . for a hundred dollars. A hundred dollars! Can you believe it?"

"Friend of mine is a veterinarian. I'll see if he can hook us up with a trap."

"Reece Montgomery, you're my hero! And let me tell you something, young man . . . you're lucky I'm not thirty years younger . . ."

He braced himself, wondering what crazy joke she'd lob at him this time.

". . . because I'd run you around that flagpole out front until you agreed to walk me down the aisle!"

"Annie," he said, "there isn't a preacher in all of Virginia who'd let a sweetheart like you marry a miserable old cuss like me."

"Miserable, my foot. In my day, the girls would have had a cat fight to get dibs on a catch like you, and not just because you're a handsome, successful doctor. Why, any woman in her right mind would consider herself blessed to have a husband like you."

Not likely, Reece thought, remembering the reasons Dixie had cited on the day she'd dumped him.

"If you haven't already done it," Annie continued, "you need to get down on your knees to thank the good Lord for chasing off that golddigger before you said 'I do.' She's trouble with a capital T, that one."

"So you're a mind reader now, too, are you?"

"Don't need to be a mind reader to know how hard it is for you to let go of things. And people. Even that poster girl for narcissists."

He couldn't deny that Dixie had been high maintenance, but a classic narcissist?

"I also know that you don't like it when people stick their noses into your personal life."

But that's just what you're fixin' to do, isn't it, Annie?

"You're not gettin' any younger, y'know. Stop fixating on the once-burned-twice-shy adage and get busy looking for a sweet young thing who loves kids as much as you do, who'll treat you with the respect you deserve, unlike that . . . that *fiancée* of yours."

Before he could puzzle out why Taylor had so quickly come to mind, Annie cut loose with an ear-piercing whistle.

"Here's a question for ya, doc: if your pal the veterinarian comes through for us with a trap and we're lucky enough to capture the li'l trespasser, what will we *do* with her?"

"Good question," he admitted. Definitely something to consider before baiting the cage.

Maybe Taylor would like a cat to act as mascot for the inn.

He told himself she'd popped into his head — again — because of their recent conversation.

"Oh, good grief," Annie said. "Gotta go. There's the doorbell."

She hung up before he could say good-bye or wish her a good afternoon.

Chuckling, he replaced the handset in its cradle, grabbed his medical bag and started the usual inventory: flashlight and batteries, prescription pad and pen, wrapped tongue depressors and disposable thermometers, reflex hammer and stethoscope, alcohol wipes, sterile gauze pads and tape, surgical gloves and face masks, syringes and needles. He'd just restocked his supply of meds, but habit compelled him to make sure he had an ample supply of analgesics: morphine and ibuprofen; amoxicillin, benzylpenicillin, and other antimicrobials.

Satisfied he was as prepared for an emergency as possible, Reece snapped and locked the bag's brass clasp. His stomach growled, more than enough incentive to inspire the decision to skip the trip home and head straight for homemade oven-fried chicken.

He put the convertible top down and cranked the stereo, but neither the wind nor The Eagles smooth rendition of "Hotel California" drowned out the Harley-like purr of the Alfa Romeo's motor.

Taylor's brother had been the only person who'd ever asked the price of the Alfa Romeo, and to keep from being judged a blockhead by his Marine lieutenant brother-in-law, Reece didn't admit that he'd paid top dollar for the used Spider or that it cost him thousands more to have it shipped to the U.S. and an additional two grand to drive it from New York to Blacksburg.

Instead, he'd pointed out that the powerful 6-speed, V-8 Italian engine could go from zero to 62 mph in 4.2 seconds flat, the car's standard-issue Bose sound system, and the two-layer, electrically operated fabric roof.

When it came to matters of finance and planning for the future, Reece had always been frugal and self-controlled. So much so, in fact, that Margo loved to tease him about it, saying things like "You're so tight-fisted, I'm surprised you can open your hand at all!" and "You pinch pennies so hard that Lincoln cries!"

Until he bought the Spider, that is.

The reason he'd splurged on the sleek red sports car had nothing to do with looks or performance. The Spider's badge so closely resembled the Rod of Asclepius — which, for centuries symbolized healing and medicine — that owning one shot straight to the top of his bucket list, and he'd take that secret truth with him to the grave.

Eli was out front, hanging from the tire swing when he pulled up to the Misty Wolf.

"Uncle Reece!" he shouted, racing across the lawn.

Reece had barely closed the driver's door when the boy launched himself into his arms.

"What're *you* doing here? It isn't Friday, is it?"

"Well, yeah, as a matter of fact, it is, but —"

"Taylor must have forgotten," he whispered as Reece carried him to the porch. "She didn't pack my stuff or anything."

Reece gently deposited the boy beside the front door. "No, she didn't forget. She called me at the office a while ago to see if I'd like to join you guys for some fried chicken." As he opened the screen door, his stomach rumbled.

"Wow," Eli giggled, "sounds like you got here just in time!"

From the end of the hall, Taylor called "What's so funny?"

"Uncle Reece's tummy is grumbling. Better get him some chicken, fast!"

White-blonde curls framed her face, and the bright blue ribbon that held back the bangs gave her gray eyes a slightly blue cast. Her cheeks were slightly flushed, no doubt from poking her head in and out of the oven, and the turquoise earrings from the set Eli had given her dangled from her earlobes. Hopefully, she'd worn them because she liked them, and not just to make the boy feel better about his gift.

The purchase reminded Reece that she

had a birthday coming up. If she hadn't already celebrated it, he'd buy her a card. Maybe a small box of chocolates, too, to show his appreciation for —

"Last time I saw you in a shirt and tie," she said, interrupting his thoughts, "we were sitting side by side in Moses Adams' office." She wrinkled her nose, as if inhaling something unpleasant. "Remember?"

How could he forget one of the worst — and best — days of his life?

"You look very. . . ." Tapping her chin with a flour-whitened fingertip, Taylor tilted her head slightly. ". . . very doctor-like and . . . and dignified."

He shoved both hands into his trouser pockets. "Uh, thanks."

Then she pointed at the clear-plastic utensils and stacks of paper plates and napkins on the counter. "The guests have already loaded up and headed for places unknown, so please, make yourself at home."

Reece loosened his tie and unfastened the top button of his shirt. "Smells good enough to eat," he said, grabbing a golden drumstick. She'd made potato salad and baked beans, so he shoveled a scoop of each onto his plate, too.

"Iced tea or lemonade?"

She looked so cute, standing there in her knee-length shorts and ruffly top, that he almost forgot to answer. "Ah, lemonade. Thanks."

He'd known her for years. Surely at some point — at a cookout in Margo and Eliot's backyard, a summer wedding, *some*thing — he'd seen her bare feet before. So why couldn't he take his eyes off her bright pink toenails?

She pulled out a chair. "Take a load off. Unless you'd rather sit on the porch."

"Where are you and Eli going to sit?"

"Outside," Eli answered. "Maybe we'll see that deer herd while we're out there."

"Maybe," Taylor said, mussing his hair.

"Taylor says the reason they come so close to the porch is 'cause the screens make it hard for them to see us. So if we're very, very quiet . . ."

"Gotcha," Reece whispered.

Plate in one hand, lemonade in the other, he nodded and followed the boy outside. He'd only been out here once before. As usual, Eliot had been deployed — Iraq? Afghanistan? — and it fell to Reece to help Margo load up the mountain of gifts she'd received at the baby shower Taylor had thrown in her honor.

He sat facing the yard and bit into a

crunchy wing, frowning as he chewed.

"What's wrong, Uncle Reece?"

Taylor frowned a little too. "Is it too bland? Not crispy enough?"

"Are you kidding? It's perfect."

"Then why the long face?"

He held up his hands, to show her his greasy fingertips. "I was gonna roll up my sleeves." Chuckling, he shrugged. "Should've done that before I started eating, I guess."

Taylor scooted closer. "Here. Let me help you."

And without waiting for him to agree or disagree, she proceeded to do it for him. "Bossy li'l thing, aren't you?" he teased.

"There are few things I hate more than seeing a man struggle," she shot back.

He was close enough to feel her breath on his cheek, to see that her thick dark eyelashes were long enough to touch her eyebrows, to notice a dot of flour on her chin. Close enough to inhale the delectable scent that would lead him to her in a crowded room, even blindfolded. And if he leaned forward an inch, maybe two, close enough to kiss . . .

Reece didn't have time to wonder where *that* crazy notion had come from — or whether he might have kissed her — because she sat back and patted both shirtsleeves.

"There," she said, nodding proudly. "All nice and tidy."

He considered picking up his napkin to wipe away that dab of flour.

"Thanks," he said instead.

Standing, Taylor crouched slightly to ask, "Would you mind very much if I left you guys alone for an hour or so?"

To go *where*? he wanted to know.

"I thought I'd try and sew a few more stitches into . . ." She glanced in the boy's direction, and satisfied he wasn't paying attention, said, "into Eli's quilt."

He held up a drumstick, gave it a little shake. "Seems the least I can do, to thank you for the free meal." Her grateful smile was all the incentive he needed to add "We'll play checkers or something. Take your time; I'm in no particular hurry to get home."

She hugged Eli from behind. "I'll be upstairs, if you need me."

The boy faced Reece. "You staying, Uncle Reece?"

"Long as there's still chicken on this platter," he said, grinning, "you won't be able to get rid of me."

After wolfing down his meal, Reece cleared the table, and seeing that her guests had left mugs and glasses in the sink, loaded the dishwasher, too. He'd just wiped crumbs off the wrought-iron table on the porch when Eli suddenly got to his feet.

"What's that funny noise?"

Reece stood at the screen door and tried to identify the sound . . . something between a scream and a high-pitched whinny, coming from the direction of the river.

"Is that . . . is that the *horses*?"

Yeah, unless his ears were playing wicked tricks on him.

"You think a wolf got in the barn and it's eating them?"

He drew Eli into a hug. "No wolves in this part of the country, buddy."

Or were there?

A year or so ago, hikers and campers with no connection to one another filed similar complaints with the Department of Natural Resources: a dozen or so wolf sightings in the Appalachian Mountains. DNR officials blamed the similarities between coyotes and wolves for the reports, and reminded everyone that attacks on humans by either species were extremely rare. They denied having released wolves into the area, as claimed by several former employees.

True or not, this *was* black bear country.

The noise from the barn was louder now

and was accompanied by the sound of wood hitting wood. Had one of the horses kicked down its stall?

"Probably just a dumb squirrel," he said to calm Eli's trembling. "Probably sneaked into the barn through an open window or something, and now it's panicking because it can't figure out how to get out again."

Eli only hugged him tighter.

"Do me a favor and let your aunt know that I'm going down there and check things out, okay."

"Okay," he said, and moved woodenly toward the door.

Almost as an afterthought, Reece blocked his path. Stooping, he looked into the boy's fear-widened eyes. "I want you stay inside until I say otherwise. Got it?"

"Got it."

"Promise?"

"Promise."

Reece gave him a gentle hug and sent him on his way.

With every step he took, the noise level seemed to double. He wished he'd thought to grab something — a shovel or a lead pipe — to defend himself against whatever was in there, attacking the horses. *Too bad you're not an old-west cowboy,* he thought, because having a loaded six-shooter strapped to his hip would feel mighty comforting right about now.

Instead of the open window he'd described to Eli, Reece noticed that the big double doors were slightly ajar. He breathed a sigh of relief, because no way a bear or a wolf could have fit through an opening that narrow. Once inside, he spotted a pitchfork on the wall beside the door and grabbed it, and said a silent prayer that he'd see the intruder before it saw him.

The trouble, he saw right off, was in the dapple gray's stall. Millie, Taylor had named her, and he knew without her having to spell it out that this was her favorite. Eyes wide and wild and ears flat against her head, Millie had bloodied both forelegs, kicking at the gate.

All four horses were highly agitated, but he focused on Millie.

"Easy, girl," he said, moving slowly forward. "It's okay. You're all right now, and —"

And then he saw it.

Teeth bared standing tall, it pawed at the air as if boasting about having Millie's blood still on its muzzle. Reece had never been much of a woodsman, but he knew enough about the outdoors to realize raccoons didn't prowl around in the bright light of day unless . . .

Taylor rushed into the barn, breathless from her sprint across the yard. "Eli said there's something wrong with the horses?"

"Better stay away from the gate," he warned.

But that's precisely where she went. And when she saw what Reece already knew, a small gasp escaped her lips. "No," came her trembly sigh, "please, God, no . . ."

"Taylor, I'm not kidding. You need to step back."

Instead, she hooked her fingers of one hand over the top of the gate, and reached for Millie with the other. "Don't be afraid, sweetie. You'll be all right, I promi—"

Reece stepped up behind her and gently gripped her biceps. "That 'coon could have rabies," he said. "You can't go in there, no matter how tempting it is."

Taylor jerked free of his grasp and whirled around to face him, head on. "I know that!" she said, her voice thick with a sob. "I've lived out here most of my life!"

"Then you know how important it is to think with your head, not your heart. You can't do Millie — or Eli — any good if that animal bites you, too."

He'd seen that "you're so *mean!*" expression on the faces of young patients whose

187

pain and panic made them a danger to themselves and those attempting to care for them. He hated doing it, but sometimes, a gruff no-nonsense scolding was the only way to reach them.

"Open that door as wide as it goes," he growled, "and get on up to the house. Call Animal Control and explain what we could be facing here, and whatever you do, *make sure Eli stays inside.*"

A minute, maybe two had passed since she'd first entered the barn, but it felt ten times that. If the heat blazing from her storm-gray eyes was any indicator, his tough-guy routine had done the trick: eyes and lips narrowed, Taylor stood trembling for all of a second, then turned on her heel and hurried back to the house.

Reece tightened his grip on the pitchfork, facing the stall with every intention of skewering the raccoon.

But it was gone.

Heart hammering, he searched the rest of the stalls, behind the feed bins, under wheelbarrows in the grooming bay, rattling brooms and muck forks as he went, hoping to roust out the masked intruder before it sunk its fangs into one of the other horses.

Shouldn't he have seen something — a flash of gray and black as it scuttled toward one of the windows or hay being kicked up by its back feet, *heard* something as it clawed its way through the opening? No . . . not with all that commotion going on in every stall.

The raccoon's behavior might be a symptom of rabies, or a reaction to being trapped in the stall with a kicking, stomping mare. After his own similar run-in with that young stallion years ago, Reece could certainly identify with that! Thinking it best to err on the side of caution, he'd snap on *two* pairs of surgical gloves when he got around to patching Millie up. Because if the 'coon's saliva got into the slice he'd picked up while digging through patient files in his office earlier . . .

No time for thoughts like that; going into the stall with the terrified horse was more than scary enough.

He couldn't count on Animal Control to get here quickly, so Reece ran to the car for his medical bag. As his grandfather always said, horses were accidents waiting to happen. Nicked shins, scraped shoulders, and abrasions caused by roughhousing or scratching an itch made it necessary to keep a ready supply of iodine, medicated ointments, and sticking plaster on hand. No doubt Taylor had a well-stocked kit out here someplace.

Sure enough, he found syringes, antibiotics, ointments, and a suture kit in the small fridge under the tack bench. Reece knew how to dose his human patients, based on weight and metabolism, but how much lidocaine was too much — or not enough — to dull *Millie's* pain while he stitched up her cuts and bites?

Taylor would know, and he could ask her . . . if he hadn't chased her out of her own barn. Yeah, he'd done it for her own good, but that didn't make it any easier to picture the way she'd looked when he snarled at her. Feelings of guilt and exasperation merged as he flipped open his cell phone. He added frustration and fear to the mix as he dialed her number.

She silenced the second ring with a curt "Animal Control is on the way."

"Good. Good." Reece drove a hand through his hair. "Is somebody up at the house — Tootie or Isaac or a guest, maybe — who can stay with Eli? Because I need you to get back down here, fast."

He heard her sharp inhalation of air. "Why? What's wrong *now*?"

"I'll need your help, keeping Millie calm while I clean and stitch up those cuts." She started to say something — probably that

190

she could do all that herself — but he cut her off. "It's only because I'm in surgery three, four times a week that I know I can get it done faster than you can." *And you're wasting precious time, Taylor, coddling your ego.*

"Be there in thirty-two seconds."

Reece figured it took five seconds to hang up the phone and look at his watch, and started the countdown at six. With every tick as the second hand swept around the dial, he found himself hoping she really *had* timed herself, running from the house to the barn. ". . . twenty-eight, twenty-nine, thirty," he whispered to himself, "thirty-one —"

"I see you found the first-aid kit," she said, snapping on a pair of gloves.

"Better make it two pair," he said, sliding into a pair of his own.

Her hands hovered above the dispenser, but only for the nanosecond it took to figure out why. "She seems much calmer than when I left here. Alvin and Bert and Elsie, too." She loaded a hypodermic with Metronidazole and added "How'd you accomplish that, Mr. Scared of Horses?"

"Hypnosis."

One well-arched brow rose as she thumped the vial.

"It's part of my stand-up act," he added. And she grinned. Not much, but enough to give him hope that later, when things calmed down, she might accept his apology.

"I told the guy on the phone they should drive straight to the barn. Let's hope they pay attention . . . and follow directions."

"So what can I do to steady her while you —"

"Nothing."

After the way he'd talked to her earlier, he could hardly complain about her tone. He stood back as she opened the gate and eased into the stall, muttering in low, slow syllables as she went. If Reece didn't know better, he'd say Millie's eyes welled up with tears as she tucked her nose into the crook of Taylor's neck. And barely flinched as her mistress inserted the needle.

"Take this," she said, holding up the needle, "and put it in that bucket near the door. Then gather up whatever you'll need to clean her up, and I'll hold her steady while you work your magic."

One thing was certain: Taylor Bradley could give as good as she got. He'd think twice — no, three times — before picking a fight with her again!

"So where'd the little beast go?" she asked while he carried out her instructions.

"Don't know." Reece poured iodine onto a wad of cotton, and got down on one knee. "Only place I didn't look was up in the loft."

Millie snorted quietly as he dabbed at her cuts, but made no move to kick or stomp him. Remarkable, he decided, that Taylor — who probably didn't weigh a hundred pounds with a full Thanksgiving dinner in her belly — had no trouble controlling a nine-hundred-pound, thirteen-hands-high animal. And kept right on controlling her until Reece had cleaned up every nick. "Now that the blood is gone, it doesn't look like I'll need to stitch anything up."

"Did you hear that, girl? The doctor says he won't need to poke you full of pinholes."

Millie's nudge nearly knocked Reece onto his butt. "Is that your way of saying thanks?" he asked her. " 'Cause if it is, I'm way okay with you skipping the formalities altogether."

Taylor's laugh was missing its usual music, telling him that she understood that Millie was far from out of the woods. Living in mountain country, he had no doubt that the horse had received routine rabies vaccinations. Unfortunately, in way too many cases, the inoculation masked the symptoms, adding to the consensus that the only typical thing about rabies was that nothing about it was typical.

The only way to know for sure if the horse had been infected was to capture and euthanize the raccoon to test its brain and saliva for evidence of the virus. If by some miracle the Animal Control officers found it, Taylor would have to quarantine Millie until the lab results came in. If AC didn't find the 'coon, the horse would remain isolated while Taylor watched for telltale signs of the disease. Either way, the coming weeks wouldn't be easy on her, so Reece decided then and there to spend a lot more time at the Misty Wolf.

"I wonder how Eli is doing."

"Wondering what's going on out here, I imagine," he said, gathering soiled gauze and cotton pads. He walked them to the bucket where he'd put the syringe. "But I'm sure he'll be relieved to hear the horses weren't gobbled up by a wolf or a bear."

Taylor closed the gate and joined him at the tack bench. "A wolf or a bear? Where would he get such an idea?"

"He's four. And a boy." Reece smiled. "A miraculous combination that pretty much guarantees that even when he's fast asleep, his imagination is wide awake."

As she put the first-aid kit to its proper place, he noticed that her hands were still shaking. It made him want to hold them . . . right before drawing her close in a comforting hug.

"You sound awfully sure of yourself." She glanced at Millie, still pacing in her stall. "I hope she settles down soon. All this excitement can't be good for her. Especially if . . ."

Especially if the 'coon had rabies, he finished silently. The virus attacked the central nervous system, so it wasn't far-fetched to assume all this agitation could speed the onset of symptoms.

He chose to respond to her first comment rather than heighten her fears about Millie's behavior. "I know it's hard to believe, but I was a dreamy-eyed kid once upon a time, too."

When she fixed that big-eyed gaze on him, his knees went weak and his heart beat double-time. What was she looking for? he wondered. Proof that he'd been a lot like Eli when he was a boy?

"It isn't hard to believe," she said softly. "I've seen photographic evidence of it. And you know what?"

Every muscle tensed as he waited to hear *what.*

"Eli favors you. A lot. Same eyes, same smile."

Her voice trailed off, and because he

didn't know how else to explain it, Reece blamed the madness of the past half hour for the tears in her eyes. Taylor faced the stall again, and as she stroked Millie's nose, he walked up behind her, taking care to leave a good two feet between them.

She'd suffered more losses than he had: her parents, then the grandparents who'd raised her, a young husband, her brother, and finally, Margo. Taylor had given new meaning to the word bravado, but he only had to blink to see the way she seemed to melt to the earth as Margo's casket disappeared into the cavernous black hole. If it hadn't been for Isaac on her left and Tootie on her right, Taylor would have done just that.

Memory of the things he'd said made Reece hang his head. He never would have admitted it at the time, but his behavior had shamed him to the soles of his shoes. And that was before he'd figured out that her heart was bigger than her head! Man, it was tempting to wrap his arms around her, beg her forgiveness, and tell her everything would be all right . . . that he'd *make* everything all right!

"I think it's okay to leave her now," he said, surprised at the gravelly tone of his voice. Reece cleared his throat. "At least long enough to check on Eli. I mean, I'm sure he's fine, but his little head must be full of questions. And —"

"You'll stay a while, won't you? Help me explain things to him?"

The two feet that had separated them dwindled to one, and as she stood looking up at him with those too-big-for-her-face hopeful eyes, he nodded. "You know I will. But . . ." Reece licked his lips, slapped a palm to the back of his neck, shook his head. "But first . . . about the way I barked at you earlier . . . I hope you'll accept my apology, because —"

She held up a hand, traffic-cop style. "Hey, I'm the first to admit that I was behaving like an irrational child. In your shoes, I'd have done the same thing." Grinning, she gave him a playful shove, then faced Millie again. "Better a firm scolding than what guys in the movies do to hysterical women."

The very idea rocked him. Had that tongue lashing at Margo's grave made him look like the type who could slap a woman, for *any* reason?

"I . . . I hope you know I'd never hurt you."

Taylor was fussing with the horses when she said, "Oh, quit your worrying. I got your number years ago."

What in blue blazes did *that* mean?

"All bark, no bite." She jiggled the stall gate to check the latch. "Why, I'll bet you can't even bring yourself to squish spiders and beetles, can you?"

As a matter of fact, he preferred the capture-and-release system. He might have admitted it, if the Animal Control van hadn't pulled up outside the barn just then.

Following the customary introductions and interrogation, each man donned thick gloves and grabbed a catch stick. If, after a thorough search, they couldn't find the raccoon, they agreed to bait a have-a-heart trap. The one in charge promised to share their conclusions before heading back to town to file their report.

Taylor started to follow them, stopping long enough to say "I don't want to take the chance they'll get Millie and the others all riled up again." Walking backward, she added "Thanks for hanging around. There's pie in the pantry. Apple and cherry. Help yourself."

And with that, she disappeared into the barn.

So much for the out-of-sight-out-of-mind maxim, he thought as, head down and hands pocketed, Reece walked toward the house.

Something told him he'd see her pretty, concerned face every time he blinked.

And in his dreams.

11

The day after the raccoon attacked Millie, Taylor rescheduled every guest, and to thank them for their courteous cooperation, promised to add three free days to their new reservations. Those who'd stayed with her before were so saddened when they heard what had happened to their favorite trail horse that they refused the offer, and all but one first-timer followed suit. Their kind words and offers to pray for Millie touched Taylor so deeply that she decided to follow through on the proposal anyway as they checked out of the Misty Wolf.

With one less item on her Worry List, Taylor wondered how she'd spend her nights. Her conscience wouldn't allow her to ask Tootie or Isaac to keep an eye on Eli while she watched over the horse; didn't feel right about leaving Millie with either of them while she tended to Eli. So she drove into town and bought a baby monitor. "I'm almost five years old!" he complained when she set it up. But he saw the sense in it when she explained how it would allow her to be in two places at the same time.

That first night, when Isaac saw her hunched over the tack bench, adding squares to the quilt, he stomped from the barn, muttering about eyestrain and backaches. When he returned a few minutes later, balancing a lamp and an end table atop one of the rocking chairs from the front porch, she wrapped him in a grateful hug.

Every night of the two weeks since, after listening to Eli's bedtime prayers, she'd gone straight to the barn. The steady sound of his restful breaths, sighing through the receiver, had a calming effect on Millie. On Taylor, too, as she snipped patches from the shirts and skirts that had belonged to Eli's loved ones. Tidy, color-coordinated stacks sat on her chairside table, their count dwindling by one every time she connected a square to those already put into place by her mother.

Yes, Eli's gift was definitely beginning to take shape. And yet . . .

By the time she'd reached this point with other quilts she'd designed and sewn, anticipating what it might look like when finished kept her sewing, despite burning eyes and sore fingers. But this one? This one left her with the sense that she'd overlooked something . . . something fundamental. Wondering what it might be preoccupied her thoughts often enough to justify the playful taunts of Isaac and Tootie. She found herself dreaming about it, too, and on more than one occasion, the question woke her in the middle of the night.

So tonight, in the hope of getting to the bottom of it, Taylor carpeted the barn floor with an old blanket and laid the quilt on top of it. She examined it from every angle — standing, sitting, even on her hands and knees — but the puzzle remained unsolved. How could she continue working on the project — her most significant to date — without figuring it out?

Frustration drove her inside. Maybe a little time and distance would give her the perspective needed to solve the puzzle. There were plenty of other things she could do while watching for signs that Millie had contracted the deadly disease, like adding photos to Eli's album or transferring all those magazine clippings to cards in her recipe file.

She kicked off her flip-flops and fired up the burner under the tea kettle. Why not make a list of chores while waiting for the water to boil? Paper and pen in hand, Taylor sat at the table, in the very chair Reece had occupied earlier. What a pity, she thought, that it took something as grim as Millie's situation to encourage his twice-weekly attendance at supper. Eli loved spending all that extra time with him, and to be honest, Taylor enjoyed his company, too.

A soft hissing sound, followed by something cool, slithering onto her bare foot, inspired a tiny squeal of fright. On her feet, she backed away from the table, looking for a weapon of some sort to defend her from the garter snake that had somehow snuck into the house.

Then she saw that it wasn't a snake at all, but Reece's tie, puddled on the floor. Laughing at the silliness of her reaction, she picked it up, remembering how he'd draped it over the back of the chair to keep it out of the gravy. Eyes closed, she pressed it to her cheek and inhaled a scent she could only describe as manly.

The teapot whistled, opening her eyes *and* her mind: she'd included snippets of Margo's wedding gown and Eliot's pleated tuxedo shirt, the pocket of her grandmother's calico apron and the bow tie her grandfather wore as president of the Parrott

River Savings and Loan. Why, she'd even included a scrap from her prom gown. All that and more, yet she'd forgotten to stitch pieces of *Reece's* past into the story of Eli's life!

Taylor took care to fold the tie and tuck it into a plastic zipper bag. On his way out the door, he'd told Eli that he'd see him tomorrow. So once the dishes were done and Eli was tucked in for the night, she'd see how he felt about contributing the tie for inclusion in Eli's quilt.

The invitation was sure to raise questions in his mind, such as why she'd decided to make the quilt in the first place, and why she felt it necessary to hand-embroider descriptive captions on every square.

Their every-other-weekend exchanges hadn't exactly been warm, but thankfully, it had been months since he'd aimed that icy green glare in her direction. And since Millie's attack, things had gone from good to better, and polite cordiality now felt more like affection — strictly of the family kind, of course!

She'd probably never fully understand the reasons for his former crusty behavior, but did it really matter, now that it seemed he'd buried the hatchet?

Then, as she stirred honey into her tea, a

thought that was anything but sweet popped into her head: would he dig it up again once she admitted the reasons that had inspired Eli's gift?

The question shadowed her as she fed and watered the horses, while she cooked and baked casseroles for the church social on Saturday, and added another square to the quilt. It was a risk she had to take, Taylor decided as she set the table for supper, because how could she call Eli's gift complete without a few contributions from his uncle!

The jangling of the phone startled her so badly that she dropped a handful of silverware.

"It's me," Reece said when she picked up.

That he'd been calling enough to expect she'd know who "me" was sent a tremor of joy through her.

"Got an emergency call, and I'm on my way to the hospital. 'Fraid I won't be able to make it for supper."

"Oh. Sorry to hear that." And hearing the strain in his voice, she added, "I hope it's nothing serious."

"Me, too."

Did the edginess in his voice mean the emergency involved someone close to him? Maybe Annie, the elderly neighbor Eli talked so much about, or Maureen or Gina, who'd become far more than mere employees over the years.

"It's Randy," he said, answering her unasked question. "His mom was a mess when she called me, so say a prayer for her, will you?"

"Of course I will." *And one for you, too,* she thought, *so you'll know how to help Randy once you get there.*

She heard the blare of a car horn and the wail of a distant siren. "I'd better let you go." The last thing any of them needed was for Reece to get into an accident because he was distracted by a cell phone call.

"I was hoping to talk to Eli, just long enough to explain —"

Another horn blast silenced him.

"Maybe you're right," he continued. "I'd better concentrate on getting to the ER in one piece."

"Don't worry, I'll think of a way to explain why you can't be here. But I won't tell him about Randy . . . yet."

"Good. Good. No point getting him upset until we know more. Call you when I can."

She was still staring at the receiver when Eli darted into the room.

"Won't tell me *what* about Randy?" he asked, plopping into his chair.

206

Help me, Lord, to divert him from the truth.

"I'm going to have to put a bell around your neck, young man," she said, collecting Reece's plate and silverware. "You scared me half to death just now!"

Grinning, he folded his paper napkin, accordion style. "Next time," he said, opening and closing the imaginary bellows, "I'll say 'jingle jingle.' "

"Better still," she said, opening the fridge, "pay attention to the . . ."

". . . 'no running in the house' rule," they said together.

Laughing, Taylor said, "Chocolate milk or white?"

She'd made his favorite: Hot Dog Surprises — baked wieners, sliced long ways and topped with mashed potatoes and sliced cheese. Maybe that would dull the sting of missing out on another evening with Reece . . . and further distract him from questions about his buddy.

"Chocolate." And then he sat back and crossed both arms over his chest. "Randy is in the hop-sital again, isn't he?"

"Yes, I'm afraid he is." The poor kid had been in and out of LewisGale a dozen times in the past year. Taylor could only imagine how it must be for his mom, wondering every time the ambulance sped toward

South Main if this would be Randy's last trip. While pouring syrup into Eli's favorite Snoopy mug, she asked God to watch over Mrs. Clayton *and* her fragile little boy.

She put supper on the table, and as she cut his hot dog into bite-sized chunks, her own little boy sat up straight.

"Is it okay if I say the blessing tonight?"

"Of course it is!"

The minute she took her seat, he bowed his head and folded his hands. "Dear Jesus, thank You for this food, and the stove where Taylor cooked it, and for giving us a house to keep it in. Please don't let that ol' raccoon have made Millie sick, and don't let anything bad happen to Randy either. And thank You for loving us, 'cause we love You, too, *lots.* Amen."

Frowning, he picked up his fork. "How was that?"

"It was perfect. Beautiful, in fact. So what's up with that sad face?"

Shoulders drooping, he shaded his eyes. "Just . . ." Sighing, he speared a bite of hot dog. "Just . . . there's a lot of bad stuff happening these days." He looked at Taylor. "What's up with *that?*"

What possible answer could she give to explain what *she* didn't even understand! "I know, and it can be troubling and sad,

208

can't it?"

He gave a lazy nod and poked at his mashed potatoes.

It wasn't like him to dawdle over *this* meal, and she read it as proof that hearing about Randy's hospitalization had upset him more than he'd said. "See, the upsetting things of the world . . . they're just some of the reasons we're so blessed to have God in our lives," she said, blanketing his hand with her own. "He promised always to watch over us."

His hand felt limp. And warm. Far too warm, even for the sticky late-June heat. Besides, the air conditioner was humming efficiently, and she'd set the thermostat at seventy-two degrees, just this morning.

Taylor gave his hand a little squeeze. "You feelin' okay, little man?"

"My head hurts." Leaning back in the chair, he closed his eyes. "My tummy, too."

Last night in the barn, the sounds of tossing and turning crackled through the baby monitor, causing Millie to bob her head. But because he quieted down so quickly, she'd dismissed it as the after effects of too much ice cream after supper. Now she wasn't so sure.

Taylor scooped him up and held him close. "What say we tuck you in a little early tonight?"

The fact that he didn't utter a word of protest scared her, but not half as much as the way he begged her to turn off the light, then flopped around like a rag doll while she changed him into his PJs.

She took his temperature, not to find out if he had a fever — because his hot, clammy skin had already made that evident — but to help her decide whether or not to give him a children's dose of acetaminophen. By itself, the 102.1 reading wouldn't have worried her all that much, but combined with the sleepiness and head- and stomach-aches . . .

If only she'd paid more attention to the news story she'd heard day before yesterday!

She'd been on her hands and knees in the rose garden when the rich-bodied voice of the DJ spoke of several Virginia Tech students who were in serious but stable condition at area hospitals after being diagnosed with bacterial meningitis. Authorities were urging anyone with similar symptoms to see their doctors, immediately. And while she tried to remember if the illness was a cold-and-flu season disease, Taylor had missed the warning signs. Not a really big deal, she'd told herself, since the campus was a good twenty-minute drive from the inn.

She left his door ajar and tiptoed to her room across the hall. It took less than a second to locate and punch the key that automatically dialed the pediatrician's number. During the first ring, she remembered how Isaac and Tootie had teased her, saying that only obsessive-compulsive types wasted their time on things like alphabetizing their spice racks and pantries, color-coding their closets, *and* storing every number in her personal directory into every phone in the house. As she listened to the second ring, Taylor thanked God. If not for her worrywart tendencies, she'd be in the kitchen right now, unable to hear if Eli's uneven breaths calmed . . . or grew more ragged.

"I don't mean to sound like an overprotective fusspot," she said when he answered, "but Eli has a fever." Taylor added the rest of his symptoms and wondered aloud if Eli might somehow have been exposed.

"He's a healthy kid," the doctor assured, "so that isn't likely."

More to quell her fears than for any reason, he rattled off a list of things to watch for: a sharp rise in temperature, vomiting, confusion, a rash, seizure. "Any of that happens, don't hesitate to call me," he said before hanging up.

Taylor sat on the edge of her bed and clutched the phone to her chest. "He's such a sweet little boy, and he's already been through so much. So please, *please* Lord, don't let him —"

The phone rang, startling her so badly that she nearly dropped it on the floor.

"Me again," Reece said.

She'd heard him angry and sad and tense, but this? "What's wrong?"

"It's Randy. Makes no sense. For a dozen reasons. And I have no idea how he was exposed, but . . ."

Taylor gripped the phone so tightly that her fingers ached. *No,* she prayed, *please, Lord, not* —

". . . meningitis. Meningococcal meningitis. He's burning up with fever and talkin' out of his head."

"The poor kid," she said. "As if he doesn't have enough to contend with."

She heard Reece's ragged sigh. "No kidding. The Duchenne's is already complicating things."

Taylor had read up on Duchenne's Dystrophy as soon as he and Eli met, to make sure that when Randy was visiting the inn, she'd know the difference between normal little boy silliness and the spasmodic characteristics of the disease. According to her research, Randy's type of Muscular Dystrophy made him far more vulnerable than other kids to everyday maladies . . . one of many reasons why kids with MD rarely lived past twenty.

"But he'll be okay, right? You can prescribe antibiotics and —"

"We're doing everything we can, but I don't know, Taylor. I really don't know." Another raspy sigh.

"How awful," she whispered. "His mom must be out of her mind with worry."

"Oh, she's beyond out of her mind. I had to talk the ER doc into giving her a mild tranquilizer."

"Poor Randy. And Eli . . ." She stepped into the hall to listen. Sure enough, his breathing sounded more labored than before. "And Eli isn't feeling well tonight either."

"What do you mean?"

A statement, she noted, not a question. In other words, he expected a detailed explanation.

"I called Dr. Sanders, and he doesn't think there's reason to believe it's —"

"Wasn't Eli over at Randy's, day before yesterday?"

"Yes." *And Randy was* here *the day before that.* Taylor closed her eyes, terrified that

Reece would confirm her worst suspicions.

"Tell me exactly what you told Sanders."

She told him about Eli's headache. The upset stomach. How he'd asked her to turn out the lamp on his nightstand because the light hurt his eyes.

"You've gotta get him over here, right now," he said. "I'd come get the both of you, but that's a waste of time." He cleared his throat. "You know where LewisGale is, right?"

"I think so."

"Just off South Main."

This calm, no-nonsense tone must be his "doctor's voice," she thought, but because matters of law and ethics prevented him from treating Eli, she'd never heard it.

"I'll use my GPS," she said. Then, "Any guesses as to how long it'll take? I mean . . . would it make more sense to call an ambulance?"

"No. That'll only scare the poor kid half to death. This time of night, shouldn't take you more than twenty minutes. I'll meet you at the ER entrance."

It felt so good, so reassuring to know he'd be there, waiting for them, that she hardly noticed that he hung up without saying good-bye.

12

Reece stood in the hall and held onto Mrs. Clayton, mostly because he knew if he let go, she'd crumple to the floor like a marionette without her puppeteer. She'd been a widow for most of Randy's life, so this latest scare was tough on her. He got that. But she had a waiting room full of concerned relatives right down the hall, whose very presence indicated their willingness to dispense physical and verbal comfort like medicine. So why had she chosen *him* for this?

He held her at arm's length and said, "Waiting is the hardest part, I know, but you've got a big, loving family." Then he took another step back, pulled the stethoscope out of his lab coat pocket, and draped it around his neck . . . a subtle reminder that he was a doctor. With other patients to see.

Thankfully, she got the message. Nodding, she said, "You have my cell number, right?"

"I do." Beyond that, what more was there to say? *Get some rest. Get something to eat. Get back to your family so I can get to* my son.

Reece hurried toward the elevators, checking his watch as he went. He punched the down arrow hard enough to make him wince. Penance, he decided, for not staying with Mrs. Clayton longer.

The doors hissed open and he stepped into the empty car, thumbing the number 1 as they hissed shut again. Would it be *nice* if his bedside manner included hugs and pats on the back? Probably. Would he be a better surgeon if he took time for long, personal conversations with his patients and their families? Probably not. If an activity or discussion didn't help him zero in on a problem or a solution, what was the point?

He'd just turned eleven when his parents volunteered for their first missionary trip to Rwanda. By the time he was eleven and a half, their angry landlord informed Reece that the rent money was gone. The news, together with final notice envelopes the mailman had been delivering, made it clear who was in charge now. A few shattered plates, a thousand bellowed curse words, and two sleepless nights later, he came to the conclusion that only three things were important in life: keeping up his grades, keeping food in the fridge, and keeping a roof over his and Margo's heads. His grueling schedule helped him reach those goals, year after year. Helped him earn full scholarships to the University of Virginia and the Johns Hopkins School of Medicine, too. But working two jobs — sometimes three — left barely enough time for sleep, let alone the "warm fuzzies" Margo seemed to need so much of.

He checked his watch as the elevator delivered him to the first floor. If he knew Taylor, she'd kept the pedal to the metal all the way from the Misty Wolf to the center of Blacksburg. He'd promised to meet her at the ER entrance; for all he knew, making nice-nice with Mrs. Clayton had cost him that chance.

Jaws clenched, he stomped up to the reception counter. *You catch more flies with honey,* he reminded himself. Forcing a smile, he said, "Has anyone checked in a boy named Eli Montgomery?"

He watched the clerk's gaze flick from his face to his ID badge to the name, embroidered in red script on his breast pocket. "Sorry, Dr. Montgomery, not here at my station," she said, standing. "Let me check with the other girls."

While she was gone, Reece faced the wide bank of sliding doors. In the distance, the flashing strobes of an ambulance sliced through the darkness. Then a squad car screeched up to the curb, its passenger door open. The cop's feet hit the pavement before the car stopped. In his arms, what looked like a load of dirty laundry turned out to be a tiny, bloody girl.

"We need a gurney!" he shouted. And spotting Reece, he said, "Hey, doc, this kid's in bad shape." With a jerk of his head, he indicated his partner. "More on the way. Bad pileup on 460."

He said more, lots more, but Reece only heard 460, the route Taylor would have taken to save time.

Another two more cops raced inside, both carrying kids. The flashing lights of additional emergency vehicles lit the parking pad like the Fourth of July. Sirens wailed. People shouted. The glint of fluorescent light sparked from IV poles. Sheets fluttered and lab coats flapped as doctors and nurses ran toward the doors. *Sweet mother of God,* he thought as he moved toward the first cop, *let her be here already.* Heart hammering, he peeled back the bloody blanket and pressed two fingers against the child's aorta. "She's breathing," he said, waving a nurse over.

"Right here, officer," she said, pointing at her empty gurney. She shot an angry glare in Reece's direction, then faced the cop again. "Would you look at that? All gray-faced and weaving." She clucked her tongue in disgust. "Fat lotta good he'll be in this mayhem. Bet he'd measure one-point-four on a Breathalyzer."

Reece had put in his time as an intern, as a resident, as an attending, so he was no stranger to chaos like this. He'd encountered nurse-to-doctor resentment before, too, and blamed that for her attitude. Because no way his concern for Eli and Taylor could have made him look *that* bad.

A small hand slipped into his, and in his agitation, he shook it off. He turned, fully prepared to unload on the knucklehead who'd trespassed into his personal space in the middle of a catastrophe.

Taylor!

Relief surged through him like white-hot electricity, and instead of venting his full head of steam, he hugged her tight. "Thank *God,*" he said. "I thought . . . it was beginning to look like maybe . . ." He held her at arm's length. "How long have you been here? Where's Eli?"

"He's just down the hall a ways." Hands flat on his chest, Taylor nodded toward the melee. "We got here about five minutes before . . . before . . ."

"Before all hell broke loose?" he finished for her. He knew how strong and capable she was, but right now, in the middle of all the pandemonium, she looked so small, felt so vulnerable in his arms.

"I can only imagine what must have been going through your mind." She blinked, bit her lower lip. "There hasn't been time to call, what with all the insurance nonsense and Eli . . ." Taylor shook her head and loosed a trembly sigh. "Sorry, if we scared you."

"You have nothing to apologize for," he said, giving her a gentle shake. "You got him here in record time." He glanced toward the pastel-striped curtains that separated the ER cubicles. "They've got him on a glucose drip, right? And did preliminary blood work?"

"No, not yet. I'm sure they had every intention of doing all of that and more before . . ." Tears puddled in her eyes as she added "My heart aches for those poor people and their families."

She looked up at him again, this time

through thick, tear-spiked lashes. He watched a lone, silvery drop, tracking toward her chin, and caught it with the pad of his thumb. Even here, wearing no makeup under the unforgiving glare of harsh fluorescent lights, she looked more beautiful than any cover model or Hollywood actress.

But this wasn't the time or place for such thoughts. For such feelings. "Guess we'd better check on our boy," he said, stepping back. Instantly, it struck him as amazing — how quickly the warmth that had seeped from her little body to his turned cold.

One corner of her mouth lifted in a sad grin. "Our boy will be glad to see you."

She led him to Eli's cubicle and shoved the curtain aside. "Look who's here, little man."

Dark lashes fluttered as he tried to keep his eyes open. A tiny grin formed on his pale face. " 'Bout time you got here."

Reece dropped the side rail and sat on the edge of the bed. He was itching to check the boy's chart, but thanks to the highway emergency, the staff hadn't gotten around to making one yet. Times like these, when no one else could, what doctor in his right mind *wouldn't* take charge of a family member's case?

Fingers pressed gently to the pulse point

in Eli's wrist, Reece winked. "You want to tell me how you got here?"

A one-note giggle popped out of his mouth. "Taylor. In the Jeep, of course."

Judging by his glassy eyes and flushed cheeks, Reece guessed Eli's temperature at 103. At least. "Got a headache, huh?"

"Yeah. And my neck hurts even worser."

Peeling back the sheet to check for a rash, Reece said, "Well, at least the nurse had the good sense to give you a gown with *blue* flowers." He chuckled, though his heart wasn't in it. "And tie it in the front."

Eli's pointer finger aimed Taylor's way. "Taylor picked it. Got me a hot blanket, too."

From the corner of his eye, Reece could see her over there, shoulders hunched and hands clasped under her chin, doing her best to hold it together. "She's a pretty good mom, isn't she?"

"Better watch it." This time, the pointer ticked like a tiny metronome. "She'll give you a time out for sayin' that word."

Reece leaned forward and slid his arms around Eli. "Love you, buddy," he said. "I have to leave, but only long enough to gather up some stuff that'll help me find out what's wrong with you."

One eyebrow quirked. "You mean . . .

you're gonna be my doctor?"

"Yeah, at least until we can scare up a better one," he said, chuckling.

"No such thing," Taylor said as he passed her.

Without slowing his pace, Reece reached out and gave her hand a quick squeeze. "Back soon," he said.

Half an hour later, he delivered half a dozen blood vials to the lab. *Flies with honey,* he thought again as the harried technician labeled them. "Let me know if I can help in any way," he told her. "I'm probably not nearly a big enough 'shot' around here to pull strings, but a couple people around here owe me favors." Reece handed her a business card. "I'm happy to trade a few to get you what you need."

She stared at the card, then at him. "Is this your *personal* cell phone number?"

"It is."

The tech pocketed the card. "I'll guard it with my life. And thanks." After rearranging a couple dozen vials, she winked. "He's your nephew, right?"

"Right."

Last he'd heard, it cost LewisGale upward of two million in salary dollars for its nearly 3,500 employees. How she'd picked up a detail like that in a place this size was anybody's guess. But if thinking she had an "in" with him — and his personal life — moved Eli's blood work to the top of her list, he'd show her his bank statements and tax returns!

"Since his mom and dad died, his aunt and I sorta share custody of him."

"Yeah, so I heard." She waved an underling closer and handed him the tray. "Give those everything you've got."

The assistant frowned. "But . . . but I have, like, a thousand ahead of these."

The tech narrowed one eye. "Yeah, but like, I really don't care. Put a rush on those."

He shrugged one shoulder. "Whatever, dude. You're the boss."

She waited until he was out of earshot to add, "And don't you forget it, brat!"

Reece said, "You have no idea how much I appreciate —"

"Don't give it another thought, doc." She made a Marlon Brando face and patted the business card in her pocket. "Some day," she rasped Don Corleone style, "and that day may never come, I *will* call upon you to do a service for me."

As he thanked her, his smartphone buzzed. He'd asked the nurse in ICU to alert him if Randy's condition changed, even slightly. It wasn't likely that the change was a good one, given the boy's condition before exposure to meningitis.

He thought of Eli, lying still and pale against his pillow. Of Taylor, putting on a brave show for her boy. He'd never felt more helpless and ineffective. Oh, what he'd give for a whopping dose of the god complex nurses were forever complaining about! Not the pompous know-it-all attitude displayed while doling out orders related to patient care, but a bona fide, genuine ability to snap his fingers once and end Randy's MD, and again to cure the boy's meningitis. Snap them a third time and guarantee that Eli had not contracted the disease.

"Oh, Dr. Montgomery, thank God you're here!" Mrs. Clayton said when he walked into Randy's room. He grabbed her son's chart, first thing. Not good, he thought, studying it. A glance at the monitors confirmed it. As she stood there, red-eyed and weary and wringing her hands, Reece thought *Snap . . . and words of hope and encouragement would materialize, just like that.*

He'd been a doctor long enough to know that nothing that came from within this building would tell her what she needed to hear. He'd been a disappointed Christian long enough to know that if God *was* the merciful, loving Father every preacher claimed He was, parents wouldn't abandon their kids to do *His* work, soldiers wouldn't die in battle . . . and their young widows wouldn't grieve themselves to death. Good people like Taylor and Mrs. Clayton wouldn't be widows, either, and kids like Randy and Eli wouldn't be teetering at the edge of life.

He held out his arms, and she willingly stepped into them. "Miracles happen every day," he said. He didn't believe a word of it . . . but he *wanted* to. "Let's not give up hope just yet, okay?"

Reece felt her give a weak nod, felt her tears, dampening his shirt. Hope. A pretty tall order, all things considered.

And surprisingly, he felt the sting of tears in his own eyes.

13

She'd forgotten her watch, and the hands of the wall clock above the door were frozen on two and eight. If she wasn't afraid Reece would show up with test results, she'd head for the nurses' station to ask for a fresh battery. Then to the chapel to pray that when he did arrive, the news would be good, for Eli *and* for Randy.

Eli was sleeping relatively peacefully, thanks to whatever calmative was drip-drip-dripping from that second clear-plastic pouch into his arm. Would they replace the glucose with antibiotics if the lab results showed meningitis?

Taylor paced the small space between Eli's bed and the empty one near the door, alternately chewing her knuckle and picking the cuticle of her left thumb. During Mark's illness, she'd gnawed her fingernails to the nub and bloodied *every* cuticle, waiting for one doctor after another to analyze CT and

MRI films, blood and urine tests. It seemed the thing she'd always been worst at was the thing she did the most: wait. The Almighty's way of teaching her the value of patience?

Her cell phone vibrated inside her jeans pocket and she stepped into the hall. Isaac, the caller ID said. When she'd called to let him know she and Eli were on the way to the hospital, Taylor had promised to update him.

"Hey," she said. "Sorry I haven't called before now. It's been pretty crazy around here."

"Don't give it another thought. How is the little guy?"

Taylor rattled off the facts, surprised at the clinical tone of her own voice. She softened it slightly to bring him up to speed on Randy's condition.

"Bummer," he said. "Count on Tootie and me to pray like crazy."

There was a certain hesitancy in his voice that made her wonder how things were going at the Misty Wolf. She'd canceled all the guests and made sure that Isaac and Tootie knew better than to book any newcomers. She'd know if Jimmy had shown up unexpectedly, because he would have headed straight for the hospital as soon as he heard the news.

"Everything okay over there?"

In the silence that followed her question, Taylor knew what the problem was.

"It's Millie, isn't it?"

" 'Fraid so. O'Toole is here and wants to talk to you."

She heard the rustling and crackling and then the veterinarian's soft-spoken voice. "Sorry to dump this on you with all that's going on with Eli and Randy," he said, "but that 'coon must have been rabid."

He explained that Millie had been stumbling and swaying, and the corners of her lips had been twitching. Worst of all, she'd been biting and kicking everything in sight . . . her water bucket and feed bag, the stall.

"If this keeps up," O'Toole added, "she'll either have a seizure or go comatose. Either way, we don't have a choice, here. It's time to put her out of her misery."

It was hard to picture her sweet Millie behaving like a wild maverick. But *euthanasia*?

"Are you sure there isn't anything we can do for her? A shot or a pill or —"

"You know me, Taylor. If there was something, I'd have done it already."

She leaned her forehead against the cool

tile wall outside Eli's door. "Yes, yes I know." But that didn't make it any easier to accept the inevitable.

Eyes shut tight, she willed herself not to cry. "When will you do it?"

"Right now, if you'll give the go-ahead."

"It can't wait until I can be there? Eli's test results are sure to come in any time now, and once I know he's all right, I can —"

"Taylor, listen to me. Please. Millie's in a highly agitated state. I'm afraid she'll have a heart attack if we put it off much longer."

"But she'll be terrified without me there."

"I know it's no real consolation, but Millie is out of her head right now. She wouldn't know you from a barn cat."

Taylor turned and slid to the floor. Oh how she wanted to let the tears flow! *You're stronger than this,* she ranted. *Get up and face the music. Eli needs you. And so does Millie.*

On her feet again, she rubbed her eyes, and on the heels of a ragged breath, said, "All right. Do it."

Back in Eli's room, she stood at the window.

A half moon hung high in the inky sky and thousands of stars winked, as if they were all in on the punch line of some cruel joke that Taylor *didn't* get. On the highway outside, the tail lights of cars and trucks and motorcycles scratched thin red streaks into the blackness, while the bright white light of headlamps lit the way for people driving in the opposite direction. Traffic lights went from green to yellow to red. Restaurant signs promised fast, inexpensive food. A revolving gas station logo boasted "The lowest prices in town" and the flickering green neon of the motel across the way said "Vacancy."

Ordinary, everyday stuff . . . all of it. But how could that be when Randy was in Intensive Care, and Eli — who'd mirrored the boy's every symptom — could be there soon, and Millie was probably taking her last breath, right this very minute! Didn't the universe realize that the earth had tilted off its axis? That everything that used to be normal *wasn't* any more?

She caught sight of her purse on the nightstand beside Eli's head. A scrap of fabric poked out of the front pocket — blue plaid flannel from one of her father's shirts. If she'd thought to grab her sewing kit, she could add it to Eli's quilt instead of standing here like a ninny, staring at her own teary-eyed weak self in the mirror.

Footsteps just outside Eli's door forced

her to swap self-pity for bravado. She'd gotten pretty good at it while Mark was dying; hopefully, she could still fool some of the people some of the time.

Reece took one look at her and said, "My God, you look awful."

Taylor didn't know why, but it struck her funny. The laughter started out quiet and small, and before long, it had him looking left and right and placing a forefinger over his lips. But he was grinning when he asked if she was trying to wake the whole floor.

By now, she'd nearly doubled over with silent giggles that brought tears to her eyes. Weak-kneed and nearly out of breath, she staggered toward the sickly pink plastic chair beside Eli's bed.

But she never made it that far, because Reece stopped her. He stood in her path and held out both arms. "Taylor," he whispered, wearing something that almost resembled a sympathetic smile. "C'mere."

She wanted to go to him. Wanted that more than anything, because she could still remember how, when he'd held her in the middle of the bustling ER, the craziness seemed to melt away, leaving tranquil quiet in its space. But her feet wouldn't move, and she knew without a doubt that if she opened her mouth, only sobs would come out. And how would that look, if Eli chose that moment to open his eyes?

Taylor hadn't expected Reece to close the space between them. But when he did, every inch of her pressed against him. Maybe, if she got close enough, some of that rock-solid stability that was so . . . so *Reece* . . . would seep into her.

She heard the steady ticking of his watch, felt his heart, keeping time with it as it beat beneath her palms. If anyone had ever told her the day would come when grumpy, judgmental, all-important Dr. Reece Montgomery would be her source of comfort and strength, she would have laughed like a madwoman. *Sorta the way you did a few minutes ago.* Oh, if Margo could see them now!

The thought inspired a smirk, which spread into a slow smile. If this kept up, she'd break into a fit of giggles. Again. What would Reece think *then*? The same things he'd always thought of her, no doubt . . . that she was a ditzy, silly blonde. He'd never said anything even remotely like it, at least not out loud. And neither had anyone else, not even Margo. But even dizzy blondes can recognize scorn when they see it.

All of a sudden, she didn't feel so comforted, standing in the circle of his arms.

"Sorry," she said, backing away. "Didn't mean to fall apart that way. It won't happen again. Promise."

"Isaac called me."

That's all he said. But then, he didn't need to say more. With those three little words, he'd told her that he knew about Millie *and* that she didn't need an excuse to break down. Standing there with his arms hanging down at his sides, shrugging, he looked as uncomfortable as she felt.

"So are the lab results in yet?"

"Yeah, they are. And . . ."

The furrow between his eyebrows deepened, and that scared her.

"And *what*?"

He pinched the bridge of his nose. "Don't know any easy way to say this, so . . ." Reece looked her dead in the eye and said, "Eli has meningitis, and Randy's off life support. I figure he has half an hour, if that."

Half an hour? Surely he didn't mean . . .

Reece nodded, and she slumped onto the seat of the ugly pink chair. "But he's barely five years old," she whispered through clenched teeth. "His whole life has been a challenge. It just doesn't seem fair," she added, punching her knee, "for him to die this way."

Eli stirred and moaned quietly in his sleep.

She'd admitted to herself, not five minutes ago, that Eli's condition had echoed Randy's, symptom for symptom. Heart pounding with fear and dread, Taylor got to her feet and grabbed Reece's hand. "What's that mean for Eli?" she demanded once they were in the hall. "Tell me he isn't on the same track." She gripped his forearms. "I need to hear you say that you've ordered the strongest antibiotic on the market, and any minute now, a pharmacy tech will be in here to deliver it."

"No, he isn't on the same track. It's the same type of meningitis, but unlike Randy, Eli was healthy and strong when he was exposed. And, yes, we'll start him on —"

"Oh, thank God," she interrupted, cupping her elbows. "Thank God, thank God, thank God."

Then it hit her: any minute now, Mrs. Clayton would lose her little boy.

"I should go to her," she said. "She probably needs —"

"She isn't alone, Taylor. Randy's mom has a big, loving family, and most of them are with her now."

Nodding, she glanced into Eli's room, and again saw the square of flannel poking out of her purse . . . same color, she realized, as Millie's saddle blanket. What better way to memorialize the boy-horse friendship than by sewing a bit of that into the quilt, too? She'd nearly overlooked including something of Reece's in Eli's quilt. What else might she have forgotten?

"Won't be easy," Reece said, "breaking the news about Randy to Eli."

"He isn't dead yet. Maybe God will bless us all with a miracle."

She might as well have said, "Did you hear . . . they discovered the moon really *is* made out of green cheese!"

"Well," she conceded, "if the worst happens, we'll tell him about it, together. First Randy, then Millie, because I don't think he could stand to hear about both in the same conversation."

He pocketed his hands. "Yeah. Poor kid. As if he hasn't already lost enough."

"If the worst *does* happen today, will Eli be well enough to attend the services?"

"I doubt it. And that's a blessing in disguise, because I'm not at all convinced kids that age should be allowed to see stuff like that."

How odd it felt, and yet how normal, discussing what was best for Eli as if he'd been born to them. Odder still . . . that in the middle of it all, she noticed Eli's PJs, neatly folded and stacked under her purse, right where she'd put them after changing him into his hospital gown. Pale blue cotton with a repeating theme of cowboys and lassos and Stetsons, short sleeves, short pants . . . and Randy had an identical pair. She'd bought them after witnessing his humiliation the first time he'd spent the night and had to call home because MD had prevented him from making it to the bathroom on time. Had he told his mom about the Spiderman underpants, blue jeans and T-shirts, socks and sweatshirts Taylor had tucked into a drawer in case he spilled a juice box down his shirt or dribbled ice cream on his pants?

"I'm almost afraid to ask what's going on in that head of yours?"

His cell phone buzzed, and he stepped aside to take the call.

Saved by the bell? Because if the phone hadn't interrupted them, Taylor would have told him about her plan to turn her mother's quilt into the story of Eli's life. He'd probably think —

"Randy's gone," he ground out. "I've gotta get down there."

When he didn't hurry toward the elevators, Taylor studied his face . . . his haggard, worry-etched, handsome face. Her heart ached for him, torn between his doctor's duty and the boy he loved so much. Being the go-to guy at times like these couldn't be easy.

"Reece," she whispered, and held out her arms, "c'mere."

She half expected he'd flash that crooked smile and say something like "Thanks, but I really should go." Instead, he closed the gap between them, just as he had in Eli's room earlier, and buried his face in the crook of her neck.

The hug lasted all of a minute, then he straightened and stepped away, one hand in the air — a silent good-bye — as he jogged down the hall.

It was as Reece disappeared around the corner that Taylor noticed it . . .

. . . the cold damp spot his tears had left on her shoulder.

14

There hadn't been a lot of one-on-one between him and Taylor since his meltdown outside Eli's hospital room. Whether that was because every hour of every day seemed jam-packed with surgeries and patient appointments, meetings with the hospital board, and trips to the Misty Wolf, Reece couldn't say. That, alone, didn't explain the way she always had something to do — feed the horses, take a pie out of the oven, tack another square to that blasted *quilt* of hers. *Fine kettle of fish,* he thought, quoting his grandpa, *when you're jealous of a blanket.*

He'd studied enough psychology to recognize misplaced hostility when he felt it: it wasn't the quilt, itself, that bugged him so much as the fact that she seemed to be hiding behind it. Tonight, he was determined to force her to set it aside, at least long enough to have that too-long-delayed talk with Eli.

A quick phone call would set things in motion: Isaac and Tootie could take Eli into town for ice cream — his treat — and while they were gone, Reece would sit Taylor down so they could hammer out a plan to get Eli to open up about Randy's death. In the weeks since that sad day, and except for being a little quieter and less active than he'd been before the meningitis attack, Eli seemed almost like his happy self.

Almost.

At the mention of Millie, he'd change the subject; bring up any reference to Randy and he'd leave the room. The behavior was no more normal or healthy than dwelling on such things. But without a discussion of some sort, something like this could fester, could even cause bigger problems down the road. Taylor might be okay with the status quo, but Reece was *not*.

He was about to dial Isaac's number when his doorbell rang. *Best laid plans . . .*

If he'd known who was out there, Reece never would have opened the door.

"Dixie," he growled.

"Goodness," she laughed, "is that any way to greet an old friend!"

She flashed the dazzling smile that had attracted him to her in the first place, and it made him wonder why it had taken him so long to call it by its proper name: phony.

Dixie used her clutch to fan her face. "You're not going to make me stand out here in the hot sun, are you?"

Oh, great. First the smile, now the well-practiced head tilt. Reece stepped and let her pass. "You're a long way from New York."

"I just bought the most charming place in Blacksburg." She made herself at home on the living room sofa, and crossing one long leg over the other, added "It's a tax office now, but with a little paint, some Victorian furnishings, it'll make an adorable shop."

In the past, if she'd dropped a hint like that, he would have behaved like a well-trained lapdog, and asked what she planned to sell. If she thought he was going to fall for that, she had another think coming. And wasn't it just like her to think he'd let her waltz in after all this time and pick up where she'd left off! "What do you want, Dixie?"

"Want?" She sat forward and struck a pose, elbow on knee, chin on fist. "Why, Reece Montgomery," she said, lower lip thrust out in a girlish pout, "if I didn't know better, I'd say you aren't happy to see me."

I'm not, he thought. But "You caught me as I was just about to leave" is what he said.

She rose slowly, adjusted the hem of her

skirt, then crossed the room and picked up one of the half-dozen framed photos of Eli, arranged on an eye-level bookshelf. "And who is *this* little cutie?"

"My nephew." He relieved her of the photo.

"Margo and Eliot's son?"

"Yup."

"Why, he was just an infant when . . ."

When you took off for parts unknown with some weasel who promised to turn you into the next Broadway sensation? Without a call or a note or —

She moved closer, traced the button panel of his shirt with a long red fingernail. "Leaving you was the biggest mistake of my life. I hope you know I never *meant* to hurt you."

Again with the head tilt. Really, Dixie? Reece forced a chuckle. "You always did take a lot for granted."

Dark, perfectly arched eyebrows rose, first one, then the other as she tried to make sense of his retort. He could call her a lot of things, but stupid wasn't one of them. Any second now, that too-familiar glint in her brown eyes would signal him that she'd figured things out. But by then, he hoped she'd be long gone.

"Look," he said, taking her elbow, "much as I've enjoyed our little reunion, I really have to go."

She let him lead her back to the door. "Important doctor things, or something more . . ." She batted her eyelashes. "personal?"

"Aha," Reece said, and left it at that.

"Another time, maybe," she said as he opened the door, "when you aren't so busy?"

He could pretend that was possible, but why waste his time and hers? "Nah, but thanks for stopping by."

With the door closed and bolted, he returned Eli's picture to the shelf, more determined than ever to get over to the Misty Wolf.

"Ice cream, huh," Taylor echoed. "Whose big idea was this!"

Eli grinned up at her. "Isaac. And Tootie." He smiled at them, too.

She almost teased them, asking why she hadn't been invited. But Eli hadn't spent much time alone with them since his illness, and the little outing would probably do them all a world of good.

Waving goodbye from the front porch, she watched them drive off in Isaac's rumbling pickup truck, Eli's booster seat raising him tall in the back passenger window. These days, she took advantage of every opportunity to add to his quilt. After a scare like meningitis — and what it had cost Mrs. Clayton — a person couldn't count on tomorrow.

Seated in her favorite chair in the parlor, Taylor draped the quilt across her lap and picked up where she'd left off yesterday: a bright red square cut from her father's buffalo plaid hunting shirt. Just a few more squares, she thought, stroking the fuzzy red-and-black panel, and the body of the quilt would be finished. Next, the border, and finally, the embroidered script that would define each square.

A few stitches into the project, Taylor heard the unmistakable sound of Reece's sportscar out front. Setting aside her work, she got up to greet him, hoping as she walked toward the porch that the strain between them was only a figment of her imagination.

"Like your shorts . . . or whatever they are," he said, climbing the steps. "Reminds me of the stuff girls wore in the 1950s."

"Back then, they called 'em pedal pushers. These belonged to my mom. Found them in the attic looking for —"

"I know, I know, quilt stuff." He let himself inside, then held the door for her.

"I don't suppose you have any of your famous lemonade around, do you?"

"Matter of fact, I made a pitcher just before supper."

He followed her into the kitchen and watched as she poured him a glass. "It's pretty quiet around here tonight." He took a sip. "No guests?"

"Only three. Nice couple and their son, here for a tour of the Virginia Tech campus." She poured herself a glass of lemonade and joined him at the table. "Says he wants to be a veterinarian."

"I'm sure they'll be impressed. V-Tech has one of the best vet programs in the country."

All this, she thought, from a guy who claimed to hate small talk. If the tension between them wasn't imaginary, what did she have to lose by cutting to the chase? "So what brings you here on this crisp August night?"

Reece shrugged. "Well," he drawled, "I thought since you had to cancel Eli's birthday party, we could maybe do something big, help him celebrate the little five." He slid tickets to a Baltimore Orioles game from his pocket. "Bought a season's pass even before opening day, thinking to take him to all the home games." Another shrug. "Then one thing and another came up, and well, we never got there." Now he tapped the tickets. "But we could. Get there, I mean. If you're game." He grinned. "Pun intended."

The way he looked right now reminded her of Eli, asking for chocolate before supper or to stay up past his bedtime, as if willing her to say yes.

"You wouldn't have to come with us to *all* the games if you didn't want to." He picked up the tickets and fanned them out, like a deck of cards. "There aren't many home games left, anyway."

"Baltimore's a long way from Blacksburg."

Eyes wide, he put the tickets down again, and waving her unspoken concerns away, said, "Oh, hey, I'd get you your own room, so don't give that another thought."

Was he *blushing*? Just when she thought he couldn't possibly surprise her, he did.

"It's just that I have guests booked straight through until October, and —"

"World Series," he said, grinning.

"I thought you didn't believe in miracles."

He snickered. "Funny. Real funny."

"What I meant was, nights and mornings are when I'm busiest around here, even when there's only one room booked."

"I'm sure Isaac and Tootie could handle things for a night or two."

Probably, but she wouldn't feel right asking them to.

"You don't have to decide right now. Just think on it for a couple days. And if you decide against it, well, Eli and I will catch a game or two, and we'll figure out another way to celebrate his birthday as a family."

As a family? Is that how he saw their little threesome?

Reece's fidgeting had slowed, but he was clearly still nervous about something. If not the tickets, then what?

And then it came to her.

"I was wondering when you'd get around to this." She'd hoped to give Eli more time to adjust to life without Randy before forcing him to confront the loss. And knowing how Reece felt about letting too much time pass before Eli faced things, she'd taken the avoidance route.

"Look, Taylor, I know he only just turned five a few weeks ago, but he's tougher than he looks. He's been down this road before, with Margo and Eliot. He can take it . . . if we're there to help him deal with it."

"He was so young when Eliot died that he barely remembers him. As for Margo . . ." She couldn't bring herself to point out that his sister had left Eli long before her death. "With Randy, it's different. They had real

247

conversations, made plans, went places together." She linked her fingers together, to emphasize her point. "They were together almost as much as they were apart. They *shared* things, Reece. That's completely different from his relationship with his mom and dad."

Reece sat quietly, nodding, forefinger tapping the tabletop. "I hear you. So you're saying wait."

"Yes."

"Until?"

No matter how fiercely she scrutinized his face, Taylor couldn't find a trace of sarcasm or mean-spiritedness.

"Until no one ever gets sick or dies. Until accidents stop happening and wars end. Until the people we love never leave us. Until we don't lose treasured keepsakes."

"In other words, never."

"Yes. I mean no . . . of course, we have to teach him how to cope with loss. But he's so little, Reece. We've been where he is, you and me, but not at the age of *five*. Shouldn't we, of all people, be able to figure out how to protect him from pain like that?"

The hand that had been holding the tickets slid across the table until his forefinger tip touched hers, and Taylor prepared herself for the lecture that would follow, that love, even love as strong as theirs for Eli, couldn't shield him from all of life's hurts. That pretending they *could* shelter him, always, would only make it harder for him to cope with the next heartbreak, and the one after that.

"Okay," he said instead. "We'll wait."

Relief surged through her. Relief and a quiet awareness that she loved this remarkable, bighearted man.

"I have something to tell you."

She refilled his lemonade. "Uh-oh. . . ."

"That night in the hospital, when I got word that Randy was gone, I . . . I didn't mean to —"

"If you're fixin' to apologize for being *human,* I don't want to hear it."

"Wow."

"Wow?"

"Here I was thinking all this time that was why you've been so . . . so standoffish lately."

"My turn to apologize, I guess. I've been avoiding you because I didn't want to get into the whole make-Eli-face-his-ghosts thing."

"Why? You thought I'd behave like a pushy, unreasonable jerk?"

She mirrored his smile. "No, not even close. I guess the truth of it is, *I'm* not ready to see him through the —"

His phone rang, startling them both. He was chuckling about that when he said hello, but ten seconds into the one-sided conversation, his smile vanished like the smoke from a spent match. Taylor couldn't imagine who might be on the other end of that call — or what dreadful news they'd delivered — to change everything from the warm light in his eyes to his relaxed posture. Reece took the phone outside, and as he paced the back porch, she heard the undercurrent of anger in his voice. He could be gruff when prying symptom details from a worried parent. But this? Taylor didn't know what to make of it.

"That was my mother," he said, dropping heavily onto the chairseat. "Seems they're coming home."

"When?"

"Day after tomorrow."

"For your birthday on the eighteenth?" She'd attended half a dozen family-only parties to celebrate the date. If his sister had been disappointed by their parents' absence —

"Please." Reece harrumphed. "I doubt either of them remembered."

She thought of all the things Margo had said about Reece's hostility toward his mom and dad. In Taylor's mind, this sounded more like years' worth of hurt and resentment.

"Did your mom say how long they're staying?"

"First of all, there's a huge difference between being a mother and being a mom. The act of giving birth can turn any female into a mother, but it takes a lifetime of being there, of self-sacrifice and selfless love to make her a mom." He pointed at the phone clutched tightly in his hand. "The woman I just talked to is my mother. *You* are a mom." He pocketed the phone. "And to answer your question, she *said* they're coming home for good. But she's said that before, too."

If she hadn't been paying attention, Taylor might not have heard his compliment, buried as it was under a mountain of disappointment.

"Well, if you need a hand getting the guest room ready, I'm happy to —"

"No way. Absolutely not. They can stay at Margo's. I've kept up with the mortgage. Might be a little dusty, but —"

Eli burst into the door. "Uncle Reece! What're you doing here?"

Every note of ire in his voice, every line of frustration on his face — gone like yesterday, all thanks to a three-foot-five, forty-pound kid. Reece squatted and hugged him tight. "What? I have to make an appointment to see my best buddy?"

Frowning, Eli said, "*Randy* was my best buddy, and he's never *ever* coming back!"

As he ran from the room, Tootie whispered, "Oh my," and Isaac said, "Uh-oh."

Taylor's gaze locked with Reece's, and she read the message sent by way of the invisible thread that connected them:

Until *now.*

15

Reece sat cross-legged on the floor beside Eli and chose a Matchbox car from the dozens scattered around them. "Cool," he said, spinning its tiny wheels. "You got this one from Randy, didn't you?"

"Yeah." He rolled a front-end loader back and forth, leaving miniature tracks in the plush area rug. "Traded him a motorcycle and a trash truck for it."

Taylor, leaning in the doorway, crossed both arms over her chest and watched the interaction. Until now, she'd never put much stock in the "Man plans, and God laughs" adage, but given that she and Reece had agreed to delay this conversation, it might be wise to reconsider her position on the subject.

Reece put the car back where he'd found it. "Guess you miss him a lot, huh?"

A quick shrug was Eli's only answer.

"Does it make you sad, thinking

about him?"

He tossed aside the loader and stretched out on his back. "No," he snapped, linking his fingers beneath his head, "it makes me *mad.*"

"At Randy? He didn't intentionally get sick, you know."

" 'Course he didn't. That would be dumb, getting sick on purpose."

Reece glanced up at Taylor, who'd taken a step closer. She sat on the corner of Eli's bed and nodded. *You're doing great,* was the silent message she sent him, *so don't stop now.*

"If not Randy, then who *are* you mad at?"

She expected Eli to say the hospital. Meningitis. The nameless, faceless person who'd transmitted the disease to Randy. When he sat up and looked at *her,* Taylor's heart lurched.

Now, on his hands and knees, he squinted one eye and flipped open the back hatch on a miniature SUV. "She *said* everything would be okay, and that a whole bunch of people were praying for me 'n' Randy to get better, and God would do a miracle." Sitting on his heels now, he met Reece's steady gaze. "How come *I* get time outs for fibbin'?"

Message sent and received, Taylor

thought, remembering all the times he'd pulled back when she tried to kiss him, and how he'd stiffened every time she drew him into a hug. Five-year-olds weren't mature enough to pick up on nuance or read between the lines, so she understood perfectly why, when she'd talked of miracles, he'd believed her. What she didn't understand was why it had been so easy to lie to her*self* by pretending that his behavior had in some way been related to his recovery.

Should she get down there on the floor with them, try to explain things from her point of view? It didn't seem fair to make Reece carry this all by himself, especially when it had been her ineptitude as a parent that put them all in this position.

Lord, she prayed, *help me to know what to do and say.*

Reece got up and rolled the chair out from under Eli's desk, sat down and patted one knee. "C'mere, kiddo. I want to talk to you about something."

"We're already talking," he said without looking up from the toys.

"Eli-i-i . . ." His blunt tone compelled the boy to look up, and when he saw that big, upside-down pointer finger aimed in his direction, he grudgingly climbed into Reece's lap.

"Thanks for cooperating," Reece said. "You saved me the bother of picking you up and *putting* you into my lap." He acted as if he couldn't see the show Eli was putting on, making circles and figure eights from his wiggly fingers.

"You're a smart kid, so I'm sure you've noticed how many loving things Taylor does for you, every . . . single . . . day." Instead of waiting for the boy to agree, Reece began listing all those things. "She does all that — and more — because she loves you. That stuff about miracles and prayers? It's what grown-ups say — even to one another — when they're scared and confused and don't know what *else* to say." He pressed a kiss to Eli's temple. "Everybody wants to believe in miracles."

"Even you?"

"Even me."

As Eli leaned into him, Reece said, "I don't think there's a person in the whole wide world who doesn't wonder why some kids are born sick, like Randy was, or why rabid raccoons bite horses . . . or why the people we love have to die. All we know for sure is that sometimes, bad stuff happens, and that when it does, we need to turn to the people who love *us.*"

The only sound in the room during that

next tense moment was the tick-tock of Reece's watch.

"Why is it so loud?" Eli asked, tapping the dial.

"To remind me how precious every minute is."

Eli slid from Reece's lap and made a beeline for Taylor's. "Did you make cupcakes, like you said you would?"

Gratitude, relief, and love swirled in her heart. Chin resting amid his soft curls, she smiled at Reece.

"Yep. Chocolate. With fudge frosting . . . your favorite."

He snuggled close for a moment, then hopped to the floor. "Well, what are you two waiting for? Let's get some before Isaac and Tootie find 'em!"

Laughing, Taylor and Reece followed him out the door. At that moment, it seemed the most natural thing in the world to sidle up to Reece and slip her arm around his waist and to move closer still when he draped an arm across her shoulders.

"You were amazing in there."

"Aw, shucks, ma'am," he drawled. "Quit it now, or you'll have me blushin' like a schoolgirl."

They'd made the landing by the time she said, "I'm serious. There's no way I could have handled it the way you did. It'll take a lifetime to make that up to you."

"Really?"

"Really."

"Hmpf. Where's a nosy reporter when you need one?"

Laughing, she looked up into his face. "A . . . a *what*?"

"You know, someone to make a record of what you just said," he said, grinning as they entered the kitchen, " 'cause I don't want to hear any 'I never said that' nonsense when I hold you to it."

"Never said what?" Eli asked. But before they could answer, he tugged the quilt from Taylor's sewing basket. "Hey. Isn't this the blanket your mom made for you?"

Her mind was still reeling from what Reece had said. "Yes, that's it."

"But . . . I don't remember this." He pointed at the black-and-red square she'd cut from her grandfather's shirt. "Or this," he said, touching the camouflage patch that had been part of Eliot's fatigues.

"Hey, there, li'l snoopy boy," Reece teased, taking it from him. "This was supposed to be a surprise." He handed the quilt to Taylor, then whispered into Eli's ear: "a surprise for *you.*"

"It is?" Eli faced Taylor. "You *are*? But

why? It isn't my birthday or . . . oh. Wait. I think I get it." He nodded. "It's for *next* year, isn't it?"

She folded it neatly and tucked it back into the basket. Giving him a straight answer was more important now than it had ever been, but how could she do that when she didn't know herself?

She could have kissed Reece when he said, "Wanna go sit in the Spider and play with the controls?"

Eli gasped and slapped both palms over his face, and when he came out from hiding, said, "Even the *convertible top*?"

"Even the convertible top."

"But . . . but it's getting dark out." He looked to Taylor for permission. "It isn't bedtime yet, is it?"

"Almost, b—"

He side-punched the air. "Aw, rats."

"— but I think since you did such a good job of cleaning your room today," she continued, "we can make an exception. But only by half an hour, because you still have some recuperating to do."

His enthusiastic thank-you hug nearly knocked her off her feet.

"You're the best, Taylor!"

They were half in, half out the door when the wall phone rang. *"Thank you,"* she mouthed to Reece. He responded with a smile — and a wink that sent her heart into overdrive.

"Hi there, Miss Happy Pants!"

Jimmy.

"What put you in such high spirits . . . win the lottery jackpot or something?"

Something like that, she thought. "No, Eli just tickles me sometimes, is all."

"Gets that from his dad." Jimmy whistled. "That brother of yours sure could tell a joke."

"Oh yeah. A regular stand-up comedian, that one."

"So the reason I'm calling . . . is my room empty?"

Taylor laughed. "Last time I checked, it said The Arctic on the door, not J. Jacobs."

"Ain't that just a big ol' bowl of wrong; as many times as I've rented that suite? I could've bought the whole inn by now!"

Another of his acerbic little quips, she knew. But Taylor didn't join in his laughter, because . . . weren't jokes supposed to be funny? Surely he realized that she got twice the money for those rooms when other guests booked the suite. He'd been Mark's best friend, and she couldn't bring herself to charge the going rate just because Jimmy could afford to pay it.

"Hey, I didn't mean to put it that way."

But Taylor wasn't so sure that was true. During their last few conversations, his so-called teasing had put her nerves on edge, and his closeness with Mark had been the *only* reason she'd let him get away with it.

"Uh-oh, I've hurt your feelings, haven't I?"

"No, Jimmy, you haven't hurt my feelings." Quite the contrary, she thought, biting back her indignation. "Your favorite suite is booked, I'm afraid, but The Great Plains and Rocky Mountain are available."

He chuckled. "I can almost see you, painting those scenes on all the doors. Which reminds me of something I've always wanted to ask you."

"Uh-oh."

"No. Seriously. This is legit."

That remained to be seen, but she waited patiently for him to continue.

"I'd understand if you called the place 'Misty Acres Inn,' since that's what your grandpa called the land around it, but why the Misty *Wolf,* with a different type of wolf on every door?"

Because when she was sixteen, her grandfather took her to the grand opening of a sportsman's supply store, where a Paul Bunyan type had displayed his menagerie.

The Bengal tiger, grizzly cub, and hyenas snoozed in their shaded cages. At first glance, it appeared the timber wolf was asleep, too. But when Taylor stepped up to his enclosure, he stood on all fours . . . and locked gazes with her. A blend of fear, exhilaration, and wonderment filled her being, and every time she'd thought of it since, that same thrilling sensation wrapped around her.

The story would only put another arrow in his Taunt Taylor quiver, so she opted to let the question go unanswered.

He filled the silence with another question. "Only reason I ask is . . . I have a gig in Roanoke this weekend, see, so is it okay if, after I wrap things up, I swing on by for a couple of days?"

"I don't see why not."

"Jeez. Could you maybe curb your enthusiasm a little?"

She could defend her snippy retort by admitting how his conduct of late had kept her off guard and defensive. If he'd let her get a word in edgewise during any one of those hot-then-cold phone calls, she would have told him about Millie. And Randy. And how close she'd come to losing Eli, too.

"Sorry. It's been a rough couple of weeks," she said instead. "How soon will you be here . . . so I'll be sure to have your room ready, I mean?"

"Last show is at eight, Sunday night, so by the time we pack up and make the drive, it'll be late. Midnight, 1:00 a.m., even."

"We?"

"Yeah . . . me and my Ovation. Can't croon a tune for my best girl without my guitar, now can I?"

She heard the smile in his voice, and it softened her heart. Slightly.

"It's awfully quiet around there, considering there's no room at the inn." He laughed at his little joke. She laughed, too, but when her enjoyment didn't match his, he cleared his throat. "So where's the pipsqueak?"

"Outside, fiddling with the controls of Reece's Spider."

In the long, brittle pause, Taylor thought she heard whispering, and she didn't want to hear whatever he was muttering about.

"So listen," she said, "between now and Sunday, will you give some thought to what you'd like me to add to Eli's quilt?"

"Me?"

"Well, of course, you."

"And Dr. Wonderful?"

O Lord, give me strength.

"Sorry. Sheesh. Sometimes my mouth is too big for my head. That was uncalled for."

Rather than agree, Taylor said, "It doesn't have to be anything fancy. A bandana, an old T-shirt . . . doesn't really matter as long as it reminds him of you."

"I have to say, Taylor. I'm touched. And proud as I can be that you included me."

"You've been almost as big a part of his life as Mark and Margo." Almost as an afterthought, she tacked on "and Reece."

In the background, she heard someone call his name.

"Time to tune up," he said. "We go on in thirty minutes."

She'd read that wishing an actor good luck is actually bad luck, which explained the famous "break a leg" cry. After all those years with Mark *and* Jimmy on the road, why didn't she know if it applied to singers, too?

Taylor wished him safe travels instead. She was promising to wait up for him when Eli blasted into the kitchen, smiling as he hadn't in weeks.

"I hate the gubba-ment!" he said, grinning.

"Now, why would a boy your age hate the government?"

"Because," Reece explained, "they drafted the legislation that makes it illegal for him to ride in the front seat."

"Silly goose," she said, heading for the stairs. "How 'bout fixing your uncle a glass of milk while I get your bath ready?"

As her foot hit the bottom step, she heard Eli ask Reece to get two glasses out of the cupboard. On the second step, he needed help getting the heavy milk container out of the fridge. Taylor froze on the third tread when he said, "Why do you have to live in a different house?"

Poor Reece, she thought, biting her lower lip. How would he answer that one?

"Because to live in the same house, a man and a woman have to be married."

"Lots of men stay here," the boy said matter-of-factly. "Like . . . like *Jimmy*!"

"Yeah, but none of them *live* here. This is like a hotel. They come for a little while, and then they go home, and someone else takes their place."

"Oh. Yeah. And plus, they have to pay money to stay here, too."

"Yep."

She heard the jug, gurgling as milk splashed into the tumblers. Then the fridge closed and Eli said, "I don't get it."

First one chair, then a second, scraped across the hardwood as they settled at the table.

"What don't you get?"

"Well . . ."

A slurp, a little-boy burp, and then, "Do you love Taylor?"

Her grip tightened on the handrail.

" 'Course I do. She's family."

"You know what I mean," Eli said.

And Taylor could just about see him, shaking his head as he said it.

"Not *that* kind of love," he continued. "I *me-e-ean,* the kind like in the movies, when guys get all stupid and kiss the girls and they giggle." He punctuated the description with an elaborate "Arrgh!"

"Oh," Reece said. "*That* kind of love."

"Well?"

"Well, what?"

He was stalling, Taylor knew because it's what she'd do in his shoes.

"Do you love Taylor like *that*?"

A heavy, masculine sigh prefaced his quiet groan. "Kinda. I guess."

Was it possible for a person's heart to beat straight out of her chest? she wondered. She could ask the doctor who was sitting in her kitchen — if it wouldn't make her look like an absolute goof.

"I think Taylor maybe kinda loves you that way, too."

Reece chuckled. "And what makes you think so?"

"Beca-a-ause, Uncle Reece, she *looks* at you the way those movie ladies look at the movie men."

I do? Taylor blinked. Swallowed . . . hard. She'd have to pay more attention to her facial expressions from now on.

"Hey, Aunt Taylor," Eli called out. "I thought you were gonna get my bath started?"

Thank the good Lord she knew every creak and squeak in this old stairway, because Taylor sidestepped them all as she raced up the stairs.

On the landing, she stopped to catch her breath and heard Eli say "That's weird."

Well, what do you expect, she asked herself, *eavesdropping like an old busybody?*

"I could-a sworn I heard her over there in the hall."

Eyes squinted tight and fists clenched, she held her breath, hoping and praying Reece would change the subject.

And he did . . . more or less.

"Me, too," he said, chuckling. "How about we split a brownie before you head upstairs for your bath?"

16

The subject of sharing houses and getting married and "love like that" didn't come up again, and at first, Reece couldn't say that was a relief . . . or a disappointment. It only took a few days, working side by side with his good-natured — if not wacky — nurse and secretary.

"I thought your parents were in town," Gina said.

"Not yet."

"But soon?"

He had a notion to show her the itinerary. And then he remembered that in her capacity as his secretary, she'd *arranged* the itinerary.

Grinning, he slid open a file drawer. "What is this . . . some kinda wacky female trap?"

"She's only asking," Maureen said, "because that house hasn't been lived in for months. And *months*. I can only imagine how many cobwebs are dangling from the ceiling fans."

"An inch of dust on all the furniture," her daughter added.

"And just think of the ring around the toilet bowls."

Gina wrinkled her nose. "Eww!"

"Okay. All right. Doesn't take a brick to fall on my head to —"

When he turned to face the mother-daughter team, he saw the foam rubber brick, dangling from the end of a red plastic fishing pole. Laughing he closed the drawer and tucked the file under one arm.

"Put that toy back in the waiting room where it belongs," he said, "or I might be tempted to give you your flu shots a little early."

"We're through for the day," Maureen said, closing the appointment book. "We could knock off early and go over there, get the place all clean and shiny for your folks."

Gina nodded. "And spider-free."

"And —"

Before either one of them could add another item to the list, he said, "They've been living in the jungle for a decade. And before that, a desert. If they aren't used to dirt and bugs by now . . ."

Maureen winked at Gina, and Gina

winked back.

"What? You two think I don't have peripheral vision?"

Shoulders hunched, they stifled a giggle.

"So how 'bout it, doc? Can we make the place all pretty for your parents?"

"Fine. Do what you please." He slid five twenties from his wallet. "While you're at it, might as well stock the fridge and the pantry."

They grabbed their purses and headed for the door. Gina stopped halfway there. "Oops," she said. "Almost forgot . . ."

She grabbed two bright lab coats from the closet — a blue one with yellow duckies and a yellow one with blue fish — and draped them over one arm. "For Eli's quilt," she said, patting them. "What're you contributing to the project?"

"Not sure." Maybe Taylor just hadn't gotten around to asking for something. *And maybe your sneering attitude last time it came up made her decide you don't deserve a spot in the quilt.* "Yet."

"Give her that weird polo shirt . . . you know," Maureen said, smirking, "the one with the fat blue stripes?"

"No-o-o . . . that tie with the reflex hammers all over it!"

"*You* gave me that one for Christmas last year."

Blushing, Gina said, "Well, gotta go. Lots to —"

Reece jangled the keys in the space between them.

"Bye," he said, shaking his head as they raced down the hall.

Well, he had time to kill. Might as well head home and get a few chores done there. Better still, he'd go through his closet to find something appropriate for Eli's quilt.

An hour later, Reece found himself surrounded by bins and boxes and cartons. An old black-and-white movie flickered in the background as he surveyed the damage he'd done, spreading the contents of the storage closet across his family room.

"*There's* another nice mess you've gotten me into," Oliver said to Stan.

"Couldn't have timed that better if you tried," Reece told himself. He slapped a hand to the back of his neck and shook his head. There had to be something among the tangle of old clothes and stacks of photo albums that would help Eli think only of him.

Then he recognized the pink box Margo used to keep little girl trinkets in. When he opened it, a miniature ballerina twirled to the notes of the "Dance of the Sugarplum Fairy," her tiny tutu reflected in the oval mirror behind her. Gently, his forefinger burrowed through the tangle of tarnished chains and faux gemstones, and there, buried under it all, a small blue envelope. On the matching notepaper inside it, Margo had written "This key opens your diary. Don't lose it!" Every capital letter had been embellished with a curlicue, and she'd dotted every *i* with a heart. He dropped the key into his shirt pocket and dug through the boxes in search of the diary — it had been pink, too, if memory served.

Ten minutes and two paper cuts later, he found it in an old patent-leather purse. He carried it to the couch and, propping his feet on the coffee table, slipped the key into a lock the size of a lima bean, and it opened with a tinny *click.* One of the biggest fights of their childhood took place when she'd started tutoring that all-in-black tattooed dropout. He'd seen the way the guy stared at Margo, not his schoolbooks, and a time or two, he'd caught her looking at the freak in exactly the same way. He'd threatened to read every page of her diary if he had to, to find proof they were more than friends. He hadn't done it, of course, because she'd locked herself — and the diary — in her room for the rest of the weekend.

And he hadn't seen it again until now.

Its cheap plastic binding creaked when he opened it. At first, the rainbow hues scribbled across the pages blurred before his eyes as he inhaled the faint scent of her favorite perfume, Tommy Girl. Finally the fanciful bubble letters took shape and formed words, sentences, and he began to read. Page after page of little-girl dreams and young woman fantasies introduced him to a Margo he never knew. He'd been too busy putting food on the table and making sure he got the kind of grades that would get him into a good college; how else could he earn enough to put *her* through a good college! If he'd known that she'd meet Eliot halfway through her sophomore year, that she'd drop out to marry him —

"Yoo hoo . . ."

Annie, come to see if he'd caught a cat in the trap, no doubt. He marked his page with the little key and opened the door.

"Good gravy!" she said. "My hearing must be going; I didn't hear the bomb that caused this!"

"C'mon in, neighbor." He cleared her a space on the couch and explained why he'd dragged out most of his past.

"What a lovely idea," she said. "I never

273

would have thought to put together a quilt for the little guy. Have you figured out yet what you'll throw into the mix?"

"Nope. I don't have a clue."

"Well, let's see if Annie Landers can dole out some publishable advice." She squinted one eye, then the other, tapping her chin with a long pearly pink fingernail. "Tell me," she said after a moment, "what was your favorite thing to do when you were his age."

"That's easy," he said. "Fishing."

"There's your answer, then. What do you have in this pile of rubbish that's fishing-related?"

Nothing from that far back, but unless he was mistaken, he still had that blue chamois shirt. When the weather cooperated, he'd spend entire Saturdays in it, jerking his grandfather's fly rod above the river. And then he'd met Dixie, who'd turned him into a yes-ma'am lapdog practically overnight. Reece shuddered. Good thing she'd never crossed paths with the guy who wrote the old "love is blind" adage, because "love is blind . . . and stupid" just didn't have the same zing.

He spotted the shirt in one of the plastic tubs. "There," he said, unfolding it. "Thanks, Annie."

"Glad to be of service. Now tell me . . .

have you bagged that ferocious feline yet?"

He blanketed the diary with the shirt. "Ferocious? What makes you say that?"

"She's been running around here for months, now, eating garbage, drinking gutter water, no human companionship, dodging those dive-bombing blackbirds. Even if she'd been someone's pet once upon a time, surely she's gone feral by now."

"I don't know about the blackbirds, but she isn't eating garbage or drinking gutter water."

Annie's pale-blue eyes widened. "Don't tell me you've been feeding her!"

"Okay. I won't." And he wouldn't tell her that the cat had walked figure eights around his ankles, or that she'd let him pet her a time or two either.

From the other side of the TV screen, Hardy said to Laurel "Isn't *this* a fine kettle of fish!"

While Annie laughed, Reece got a glimpse of the diary, peeking out from beneath his shirt. Now that he'd found the right addition to Eli's quilt, he wanted to finish reading the diary, and close the book — literally and figuratively — on that chapter of his life.

If he'd known what Margo had written on those final pages, he wouldn't have been in such a hurry to show Annie to the door.

Gina unplugged the vacuum cleaner and started winding up its cord. "I'm really glad you could join us, Taylor."

"Wouldn't have missed it for all the world," she said, spritzing furniture polish on the coffee table. "A chance to see you guys when Eli doesn't need a booster shot *and* do a good deed? How many times is something like this going to happen!" It was good to have all the hard work to distract her from Eli's conversation with Reece, too.

Maureen slid the last of a hundred books onto its freshly shined shelf. "Can you believe how much we accomplished, just the three of us?"

The threesome faced one another in a triangle, hands on their hips and frowning.

"What's left to do?" Gina asked.

"The rest of the laundry," Maureen said, counting on her fingers, "scour the kitchen sink, make up the bed, fill the fridge and the pantry."

"Why don't you two do the grocery store run while I stay here and finish up."

"Sounds like a plan," mom and daughter said and left Taylor alone in the house.

She'd spent countless hours here over the years, keeping Margo company when Eliot was deployed, babysitting Eli when his mom drank too much or took one too many sleeping pills. When Mark was on the road, Taylor had missed him, too, but she'd rather miss him than blot him from her memory with alcohol and drugs!

It didn't take long to get the master bedroom ready for Reece's parents. Odd, that he'd held onto the house all these years. God sure knows what He's doing, she told herself, because if Reece had sold it after Margo's accident, her mom and dad wouldn't have a place to come home to . . . a clean cozy place, thanks to Gina and Maureen, insisting that Reece let them tidy up.

A glance at the clock told her she'd imposed on Isaac and Tootie long enough. Besides, she had beds to change at home, breakfast to plan, a sweaty little boy to bathe and tuck in, and a quilt to finish.

After making the turn onto Turner Street, Taylor decided it would be a shame not to stop for some of Eli's favorite muffins and a few cookie crumblers, too. The short walk from the parking lot to the Next Door Bake Shop felt refreshing, despite the sticky August air.

"Taylor . . ."

The voice had come from across the street.

"Taylor *Bradley*?"

Mark's old roommate? It had been years since she'd seen Fred!

As he made his way to her side of the road, she was sure of it. "Didn't your mother teach you to look both ways before crossing the street?" she teased.

A car horn blared and a minivan slowed as Fred held up one hand. "Sorry," he said, wincing as he saluted the driver. When he reached Taylor, he added, "You know me. Never did much care for authority figures."

Which was nonsense, because last she'd heard, Fred had founded a corporation that made him famous the world over as "The Diamond Guy." And a person didn't reach those heights by disrespecting people in power.

She hugged him hello. "You look great, but I almost didn't recognize you behind all that hair stuck to your handsome face."

Grinning, Fred cupped his chin. "This old thing? Had it for a lot of years now. Guess you'd say it's one of my trademarks."

The other being diamonds, of course. "Still designing Superbowl rings and jewelry for kings and queens?"

"Yeah," he said, waving the compliment away. "And is that husband of yours still the worst taco maker in the country?"

That husband of hers had been gone for

years now, but they'd lost touch with Fred a long time before that. He hadn't heard. How *could* he have heard that Mark had died? His simple question caught her so off guard that it rendered her speechless, and the reaction showed on Fred's face.

"Aw, man. No. No way."

It showed in his concerned voice, too. "Oh, now, don't look at me that way. I'm fine." She squeezed his hand. "Honest."

"So . . . so what . . . how did it happen?" Then his hands went up, as if she held him at gunpoint. "You don't have to answer that. I'm an —"

"How 'bout we go inside," she said, pointing at the Bake Shop's door. "I'll tell you all about it over coffee."

"I'd love that, but . . ." Fred winced. "I have to get over to Virginia Tech, to give my lecture about how to tell a real rock from a fake."

"I saw you do that demonstration on *The Tonight Show;* it's the reason I wore a plain gold band." Until Eliot and Margo died, reminding her how much it hurt to lose Mark. Why wear a symbol of love and marriage when she wanted no part of pain like that again?

"I'll be in town through the weekend. Give me a call," he said, handing her his card.

"Maybe we can work something out."

"Will you be here on Sunday?"

"Matter of fact, I don't leave until Monday afternoon."

"Then come to dinner. We can sit around and relax, get caught up . . . and I'd love to introduce you to Eli."

"You and Mark had a kid? That's great!"

Now that he was smiling again — really smiling — she hated to break it to him.

"No, Eli is my brother's little boy. I got full custody when Eliot died in Afghanistan and my sister-in-law had an accident a few months later."

"Good *God*, Taylor. Life has really put you through the ringer lately, hasn't it?" He handed her a pen. "I'd love to have dinner with you. Scribble your address on the back of that card while you tell me what I can bring and how early I can get there."

She withdrew one of her own business cards from her purse and gave it to him. "We eat at three on Sundays, but you're welcome any time."

"Looking forward to it," he said, squeezing her hand.

With that, Fred walked south as she hesitated outside the café door. All of a sudden, the muffins lost their allure; the only thing she was hungry for right now was a

big hug from Eli.
And maybe one from Reece.

17

"Make yourselves at home," Reece said at the end of the tour.

"That won't be hard," Judith said softly. "It's a lovely house."

"Yes, Margo had excellent taste." *Which you'd know if you'd ever been here before.* "There are a few things in the fridge and pantry. Make a list of anything more you'd like, and I'll pick it up on my way home this evening. Tomorrow, I'll see if my secretary can —"

"You seem a little disappointed that we can't join you for dinner, and I'm sorry about that, but your dad's exhausted."

Is that how she'd interpreted his pent-up rage? As *disappointment*? That might be funny . . . if it wasn't so all-fired sad.

"You know we'd love to join you otherwise, don't you?"

Now how would he know *what* they loved, or what they didn't love, when they'd been out of the country for most of his life?

Judith looked around the room and nodded. "You certainly did right by your sister." Tears shimmered in her eyes when she smiled up at him. "You always were a good boy — we couldn't have dedicated ourselves so wholly to God's work if you hadn't been — and you're a good man, too."

Oh, this is rich! he thought. So that's how they'd chosen to rationalize all those lessons in checkbook balancing and first aid and running the household appliances . . . so they could desert their kids *to do God's work*?

"Train up a child in the way he should go," she recited, eyes closed and pointer finger aimed at the ceiling, "and when he is old, he will not depart from it."

"Proverbs 22:6." The fact that he'd remembered it after all these years surprised him. That she had the unmitigated gall to look proud of the lessons she and his dad drilled into his and Margo's heads — by any means necessary — didn't. And people wondered why he took such a hard line on Christians!

"My biggest regret is that *you* haven't given us grandchildren."

He searched her gaunt face for a sign that she'd been joking, because surely that wasn't her biggest regret. "Oh, don't look so worried," she said, squeezing his forearm. "You're not getting any younger, but it's different for men. You can have children until you're old and gray. Why, just look at Abraham!"

That was no more relevant than the fact that Sarah was ninety when she gave birth to Isaac. Yeah, he knew his Bible, all right, including Exodus 20:12. It hadn't been a huge hardship, obeying the rest of the Ten Commandments, but that fifth one? The only reason his father was off napping in his dead daughter's house was because Reece had chosen not to add an *if* to that one: *honor thy father and mother* if *they didn't leave their children without explanation and barely enough to sustain them for six stinking months.*

If he closed his eyes, he could read what Margo had written throughout her diary: *Reece is mean. Reece is a control freak. Reece cares more about getting good grades and making money than he does about me.* And the kicker, found on the last page: *Reece does what he must to keep up appearances, but he's selfish and cold. And knowing what's about to happen, I can't in good conscience leave Eli with a man like that.* Seven exclamation points followed that entry. Seven!

"I can see that you're restless . . . I get the same way when I'm worried that I might not arrive on time! So you go on ahead to your little dinner party. Your father and I will be just fine. We don't want you to be late on our account."

They waltzed in here after decades of tending to the needs of other people's children, but didn't want *him* to be late. Priceless! When Jesus said leave your worldly possessions behind and follow me, *that isn't what He meant!*

If he didn't get out of this house, and fast, Reece didn't know what awful thing he might say. Like *God's work was more important than being with your daughter on her wedding day. More important than consoling her when her husband died at war. More important than making sure your only grandchild was properly cared for after* . . . Reece couldn't complete the rant for fear he'd hate them for paving the road she'd followed to suicide.

He walked toward the foyer. "You have my cell number," he said. "When I get to the office in the morning, I'll make some calls, find a good oncologist for Dad." He stood on the porch, one hand on the doorknob to add, "I'll call you soon as I've

285

scheduled an appointment." The lock slipped into place with a quiet click as he added to his list: *God's work was more important, even, than finding out why you'd been coughing up blood for* years.

As he drove toward the Misty Wolf, he wondered how many times had they chanted "your body is His temple" lectures? Too many to count! The fact that they so rarely practiced the Word they claimed to love made them far more than incompetent parents — it labeled them blatant hypocrites, too.

Maybe he'd been lying to himself all these years, and his drive and determination to provide a better life for Margo and himself was nothing more than a different brand of hypocrisy. Calling it "protection" or "preparation for the future" didn't change what it was; the idea that his own self-righteousness might have played a part in her decision to end her life awoke guilt and self-loathing like he'd never known.

He gave a mental thumbs-up to Margo for seeing through his façade. Her decision to kill herself had been sick and selfish, but putting Eli in Taylor's loving care had been anything but.

Reece might have turned around, to bask in Taylor's one-of-a-kind care right now. He knew that she deserved better, far better than the likes of him, and *still* he wanted her in his life. Saul had been a vile, despicable man before his conversion, so maybe there was hope for him, too. The concept made him grateful that his stubborn pride kept him from admitting how he felt about her before now, because knowing Taylor, she'd have accepted him as-is.

A glimmer of hope sparked in his soul: tonight, after Eli went to bed, he'd bare his soul. If she still wanted him after hearing what a low-down miserable cur he'd been . . . if he could make her believe he'd become the man she deserved.

He parked the Spider in its usual place, and as he climbed the front porch steps he prayed, *really* prayed for the first time in years:

Her life is in Your hands, Lord.

18

"This is perfect," Taylor said when he handed her the shirt. "I've always loved the feel of chamois against my skin." As if to prove it, she pressed her cheek into it. "I'll be sure to put it close to the hem, so he can get the full benefits of its suppleness."

"If I'd known it was *that*," he teased, "I probably wouldn't have worn it fishing."

She hooked her arm through his and led him into the kitchen.

"Where is everybody?"

"The guests are shopping in Blacksburg, and Eli took Jimmy riding."

"Jimmy," he echoed. "When did he roll in?"

"About an hour ago." She hung his shirt on the wooden peg beside her apron. "The man is insane," she added, grabbing the apron. "Did a show in Roanoke that lasted until ten, then drove straight here."

Poor baby, he thought. "He's a big strong

288

boy. Besides, it's not a long drive, especially in weather like this."

"I know. But it surprised me that he put the new guy in charge of the equipment. Pete is the only one he'd ever trusted with that job."

He helped himself to a cookie. "Wonder what changed?" He'd been serious about turning over a new leaf. What better way to test it than by feigning interest in poor Jimmy's problems?

"Pete's wife just had a baby, and there were complications so he's taking some time off."

"With the wife, or the baby?"

"The baby. Anita refused that prenatal test they do to check for Down Syndrome."

"I'm sure they'll figure out it isn't all bad. These days, kids with Down's can live long, perfectly normal lives. Two of my patients have it, and they're doin' great. If Pete needs any referrals — to specialists or support groups in their area — let me know."

She sent him a crooked little smile. "I'll tell him."

"So did Isaac and Tootie go into town, too?"

"No, they're still at church." She wiggled her eyebrows. "Just between you and me, I don't think it'll be long before that man pops the question."

Won't be long before I do the same.

The phone rang, and while she chatted with the person on the other end, he poured himself a glass of iced tea. There was a pitcher just like this one in the fridge at Margo's, only that one held lemonade. He'd seen a tray of brownies on the counter, and the whole place had looked terrific. A decent guy would stop on the way home for gift cards to thank Maureen and Gina for their hard work, if his me-oriented brain didn't forget.

Taylor kept pens and tablets in the drawer under the phone, so he put his hands on her hips, thinking to move her aside without interrupting the phone conversation. No big deal. Just whisper "excuse me" and fetch the writing materials, and get busy scribbling a note.

That might have been true . . . if she hadn't leaned into him, making an odd little purring sound. *Step away from the girl,* he told himself. *Step. Away. From the girl, before you do something stupid.* Like bury his face in her soft curls, or press a kiss to her cheek and mess up the timing of the speech he intended to make, first chance he got.

She'd barely hung up when Eli and Jimmy joined them. "I didn't expect to see you two for another hour yet!"

"My bum hurts," Eli said, rubbing his backside. "Elsie is one bouncy horse!" Then he ran up to Reece, who scooped him into his arms.

Jimmy stood beside Taylor at the stove. "Something smells good," he said, leaning over the pot. "What's cookin'?"

"I know what it i-i-is, I know what it i-i-is," Eli sang. Then he cupped both hands around Reece's ear and whispered "It's your favorite. Mine too."

Spaghetti and meatballs with her one-of-a-kind sauce.

But he played along with the game. "Deep-fried giraffe?"

Eli giggled. "No!"

"Baked spiders?"

"Yuck!"

"Then it must be steamed earthworms."

"Oh, gross!"

"Sorry, buddy, I'm clean out of ideas."

"Eli," Taylor said, "how 'bout washing up so you can set the table?"

Reece put him down and he ran straight for the powder room. "I can set the table if you like."

She emptied a box of pasta into boiling water. "I'm sure Eli would love it if you gave him a hand. You know where everything is," she said, stirring it.

Take that *Jimmy Jacobs.* On second thought, that's what the *old* Reece would have said. He smiled — or the closest thing he could muster, anyway — and washed his hands at the kitchen sink. "I'll set out the glasses if you'll fill 'em with ice and water."

"Thanks, but I think I'd rather stay right here and keep the cook company."

Was it his imagination, or had the comment made Taylor blush? *Nah . . . probably just the steam from the spaghetti pot.*

His cell phone chirped, and he tossed the towel aside to answer it: one of his patients had spiked a fever, and the nurse added, the antibiotic had given the kid an itchy rash. "Give him a low dose of Benadryl," he said, "and speed up the glucose drip." He checked his watch. "I'll be there in thirty."

When he turned to let her know he couldn't stay, Taylor nodded. "Go, and be careful driving. If you're not too pooped after you take care of things, feel free to come back. I'll save you a plate."

Man, but she was gorgeous, especially at times like this, when she got all caring and thoughtful. And with her cheeks all pink and dewy from standing over the hot pots. If Jimmy wasn't standing there, thumbs tucked behind a belt buckle almost as big as his head, Reece might have hugged her.

"If it isn't too late, I might just take you up on that." He stooped to kiss the top of Eli's head. "Sorry, kiddo, gotta run."

"Sick kid, huh?" he asked.

"Yeah, 'fraid so."

"Well, he's lucky," Eli said, beaming up at him, "that you're his doctor."

He carried the compliment with him all the way to the pediatric ward, and as he made his way to Seth Carter's room, he thought about what Eli had said — that Taylor made the meal because it was his favorite. Correction, he thought, grinning, *our* favorite.

Evening was Taylor's favorite time of day.

With the dishes done, her guests in their rooms, and Eli fast asleep, she was free to carry the quilt onto the front porch and sew by the glow of lamplight filtering through the parlor window behind her. Jimmy's soft voice and guitar music sighed through the screen.

Yesterday, she'd found the mate to that old satin glove, so first order of business tonight . . . replace the missing button. What she'd do with them now, Taylor didn't know. Thankfully, no one could read her mind, because she felt a little silly, taking such satisfaction from knowing they'd been reunited after so many years apart.

With the gloves wrapped in white tissue and tucked into her basket, she picked up the shirt Reece had brought by earlier. It was soft and lightweight and the color of the sky just after a hard rain. She held it to her cheek and drank in its musky scent.

"Ninny," she muttered, putting it back into the basket. She was nowhere near ready to add a piece of it to the quilt, but even when she was, it seemed a shame to cut it up.

"Ridiculous," she whispered, tucking it deeper, so that she didn't have to look at it. Because she hadn't thought twice about taking the scissors to Margo's wedding gown, Eliot's Marine-green T-shirt, or any of the other clothing confiscated from old boxes and bins. Much longer in those containers, she'd told herself, and they'd be too threadbare to be of use, even as dusting cloths. So why had one well-worn fishing shirt taken on such importance?

The singing and strumming stopped, and she heard the familiar *plink* as Jimmy slid his guitar pick under the tightly wound strings wrapped around the tuning keys. Hopefully, he'd head straight up to bed.

But who was she kidding? He'd feel

obliged to step outside, at least long enough to tell her goodnight. "If you're lucky . . ."

"Talking to yourself again, I see."

She heard the grin in his voice and matched it with one of her own. "Only way I know to guarantee at least *one* person is listening."

He chuckled, then said, "I was just about to pour myself a glass of iced tea. Can I get one for you?"

"Are you kidding? I don't get enough sleep as it is. One sip of that stuff and I'll be up all night, prowling around the house."

"Funny. Caffeine never affected me that way."

It hadn't affected Mark either. The man could guzzle a huge mug of the stuff, put his mug on the nightstand, and fall straight to sleep.

"Men," she said, mostly to herself.

"Aw, we're not all bad."

She knew that better than most women. Her grandfathers had both been stand-up guys, and her dad had been her best guy . . . until Mark came along. She didn't think it possible to meet anyone else who'd make her feel like he did, until —

"Lemonade, then. Or will the sugar keep you up?"

"I'm not really thirsty." She wouldn't have

admitted it if she had been, because then he'd feel duty-bound to sit with her while she sipped it. The quiet was one of the reasons she so enjoyed the hours after supper.

"How would you feel about taking a walk with me?"

"A walk? Where?" But the better question was *why.*

"Just down to the barn." He produced an apple from behind his back. "Thought I'd split it three ways and give those mules of yours a little treat."

"They behave perfectly when *I* ride them," she said with a deliberately haughty air.

"C'mere," he said, extending his free hand.

C'mere. It's what Reece had said when Eli and Randy were so close to death, right before he —

"We won't stay down there long. I promise."

She'd been sitting in one position long enough that the walk would probably feel good. Setting aside the quilt, she grabbed the baby monitor and joined him.

While he carved the apple and fed it, bit by bit to the horses, he chatted about his next job, told her his agent was working on getting him a movie deal, then started listing the challenges Pete's family faced with this new addition to the family. "They don't know it yet, but I paid off their mortgage and set up a hospital fund for the kid. That way, when the insurance runs out, they won't have to tap into their savings."

"Wow, Jimmy, that's really sweet. And generous."

The apple was gone now, but he still had the horses' full attention. Elsie nosed his elbow where it rested on her stall gate.

"You could at least pretend not to sound so surprised," he said, stroking the mare's nose. "I think about other people now and then."

"I know that better than most."

Evidently, the simple statement reminded him, too, of those dark, sad days after Mark died, because he reached out and tucked a curl behind her ear.

"Only too happy to be there for you, Taylor."

"We should probably head back," she said, shaking the monitor. "I haven't heard a peep from this thing since we left the porch."

He took her hand and led her down the flagstone path that connected the house to the barn. "So you doin' okay?" he asked.

"Sure. Why wouldn't I be?"

"Because in these last couple of years

you've gone through more tragedies and traumas than any ten people I could name."

Please God, don't let him list them. Because on a night like this, with storm clouds hiding the moon and this melancholy ache of missing Reece beating in her heart, she might just start blubbering like a baby.

He ticked them off, one by one, starting with her mom and dad, and ending with Randy. Even as the tears filled her eyes, she felt like a little twit and did her best to blink them back. And darn that Jimmy! He took her in his arms!

"Bet you haven't allowed yourself to cry at all, have you?"

Yes, she had . . . both times in *Reece's* arms. She'd heard what he said that night in the kitchen, when Eli peppered him with questions about love and marriage and moving into the Misty Wolf. He'd been busy in the weeks that had passed, what with work and his parents coming home, weekends with Eli and his own place to take care of. *But you'd think he could have found one minute to say those things to* you . . . *if he'd meant them.*

"You aren't Atlas, y'know. Nobody can stand up under all that without caving . . . a little bit."

One of the horses whinnied . . . and she

thought of Millie.

The monitor in her hand came suddenly to life, and she heard Eli's sleepy murmurs, sighing through its speaker and remembered how close she'd come to losing him.

The scrap of cloth in her pocket, tucked there so she wouldn't forget to put it into the sewing basket, made her aware of the important task she'd undertaken, to ensure Eli would never lose touch with the fabric of *family*.

An owl hooted — Mark's favorite night sound. It was the last straw.

Taylor didn't know how long her pathetic display of weakness lasted, but when it ended with one high-pitched hiccup, the sobs turn into snickers that must have been contagious, because soon, Jimmy was laughing, too.

"Sorry about that," she said, wiping her eyes with the sleeve of her T-shirt. "But really, you only have yourself to blame. You should know by now what can happen when you talk about all that stuff."

"First of all," he said, "you have nothing to be sorry for."

It seemed to Taylor that he was memorizing every inch of her face, his gaze flicking from her eyebrows to her cheeks, then lingering for a second on her lips before meeting her eyes. *Better change the subject, and fast,* she thought.

"And second of all?"

One big knuckle lifted her chin. "Second of all," he whispered, "*this* should have been first of all."

And then he kissed her.

She broke free of his embrace, and fingertips pressed to her lips, took a step back. Everything Tootie had said about Jimmy — comments Taylor had shoved to the back of her mind — hurtled forward. Much as she hated to admit it, her friend had been right.

There was just enough moonlight for her to see his soft smile turn into a frown. The last thing she wanted was to hurt his feelings. But she couldn't let him think there could ever be more between them than friendship.

A car door slammed and they both turned toward the sound.

Reece.

How much had he seen?

One look at his sad green eyes told her he'd seen everything. Would he have looked that way if he *hadn't* meant those things he'd told Eli? She didn't think so. But what a horrible, crazy, *stupid* way to find out!

"Just stopped by to let you know I can't stay for supper," he ground out, "so I hope you didn't go to a lot of bother, saving me a plate."

"It wasn't any bother," she blurted. "I can heat it up in no time."

"No, no," he was saying, head down and hands pocketed as he walked back toward the Spider. "Early day tomorrow. See you Friday when I pick up Eli."

As he slid behind the wheel, Taylor wondered about God's timing. Was this His way of letting her know that a future with Reece wasn't in His plan?

Shoulders sagging, she trudged up the porch steps, with Jimmy at her heels. She couldn't hold his feet to the fire for this, because if she'd paid more attention to Tootie's advice, things never would have gone this far. Now Jimmy's feelings were hurt and Reece's ego was bruised, all because she'd been too wrapped up in . . .

Oh what did it matter *what* excuse she came up with? The bottom line was, yet again, she'd let someone down.

So that *was Your plan, was it, Lord . . . to save Reece from the same thing?*

What had he said that night in Eli's hospital room? *Think with your head, not your heart.* Life being what it was, Reece would no doubt experience disappointment and disillusionment at some point down the road, but if she took his advice, he'd have a friend to turn to when it did.

If he'd let her *be* his friend, that is.

19

It had taken longer than expected to regulate Seth's vitals, and Reece hung around a half hour after that, just to make sure the boy was stable. The thought of thick, perfectly spiced sauce and big tender meatballs made it hard to keep the speedometer at fifty-five, but he'd managed it. If he'd stepped on the gas and got there five minutes earlier . . .

He rubbed his eyes, hoping to erase the image from his brain.

No such luck. He'd probably see it for months, every time he closed his eyes.

It would have been easy to despise Jimmy, but the guy had known Taylor for most of her adult life. The fact that he'd held off this long was pretty remarkable. But then, Reece had known her almost as long. Had the singer felt unworthy of her, too? He couldn't think of any other reason the man hadn't moved in once Mark was gone.

"Well, old man," he told himself. "Looks like you can go right on being your egocentric self." He'd keep right on giving 125 percent to every case, every patient. Do the right thing by his parents. Be anything and everything Eli needed. But why put any effort into becoming a better man if he couldn't have Taylor?

What he needed more than anything right now was something to put a stop to his self-pitying thoughts.

He hadn't phrased it as a prayer, and yet his cell phone rang.

He looked for a place to pull over.

Nothing.

Reece thumped the steering wheel in frustration. That left him with two choices: let the call go to voice mail or take it, and hope the cops wouldn't catch him talking without a headset on. He gritted his teeth and punched Talk.

"Reece?"

Aw, man . . . if he got a ticket because of his mother, wouldn't *that* just be the fudge on the sundae. He snorted at the irony because it was Sunday.

"I've called an ambulance," she said. "Your father . . . he . . . it's bad, really bad, son."

Guilt, for having assumed she'd called to

shoot the breeze, gave way to a peculiar fear: his father was dying, and despite their antagonistic relationship, it was tough to admit.

"How long ago did you call?"

"Seconds before I called you."

He was, at most, five minutes from Margo's place. If he could get there before the EMTs, he and his mother could follow the ambulance to the hospital.

"I'm on my way." She'd been a nurse practitioner in her premissionary life, and the way she'd conducted herself when he'd visited their bleak little village told him she hadn't left her skills behind. "Are his vitals steady?"

"Yes," she said, "but he's coughed up an awful lot of blood."

He turned on his calm, reassuring doctor voice. "Well, you know what to do. Just keep him as comfortable as you can, and make sure the airway isn't blocked. I should be there any minute."

The instant he hung up, Reece dialed 9-1-1, explained the situation to the dispatcher, and asked her to patch him through to the ambo crew. When she did, and he repeated the essentials, recited his ETA, and tromped on the gas pedal, thinking that the next time he inadvertently prayed for a distraction, he'd take care to be more specific.

20

His mother stared through the glass-enclosed IC unit where a nurse held a spit cup under his father's ashen chin.

"Why is he refusing pain meds?" his mother demanded. "An oxygen mask, at the very least!"

Probably, Reece thought, because in his disoriented mind, he saw his suffering as something God would view as saintly. On second thought, it wouldn't take delirium to make him think that way. Twisting the Scriptures to suit himself had been part and parcel of his character. The pot and the kettle analogy came to mind as he remembered that for every verse his father fractured, his mother came up with two to back it up.

But this was neither the time nor place for such a declaration.

"The Reverend Wayne Montgomery is a proud man," he said, and left it at that.

"Pride is a sin."

He leaned forward slightly to see if the look on her face matched the wrath in her voice.

But she hid behind her hands and started to cry.

He put his arms around her and tried to remember if they'd ever been this close, physically or emotionally. Nothing came to mind, and he stood, patting her bony back and muttering useless epithets until her sobs subsided. She blotted her eyes and blew her nose, walked ramrod straight to her husband's bedside, and kissed his forehead.

It became a pattern that repeated itself, twice, three times a day, and with the passage of each agonizing hour, his father grew weaker. And yet he hung on. *What are you afraid of, Dad?* he wondered.

Reece instructed Maureen to reschedule all his appointments, indefinitely, and he called in a few favors to hand any surgery that couldn't wait to colleagues. He drove his mother to the funeral home and helped her make some preliminary arrangements. They'd never held insurance and hadn't written a will, so it fell to Reece to absorb the costs.

He hadn't taken any of Taylor's calls, hadn't answered any of her messages for reasons that had nothing to do with his father's condition. But when Friday morning rolled around, he knew he couldn't put it off any longer. This was an Eli weekend, and like it or not, he had to call and cancel it.

"Oh my goodness," she said, first thing. "It's such a relief to hear your voice! I've been trying to reach you, to explain that —"

"I'm at the hospital," he said.

Silence. He could almost hear the wheels, spinning in her head: *You're a doctor. Where else would you be?*

"It's my father. He's dying." The way that last word came out, dry and trembly and reedy, surprised him. He cleared his throat and started over. "So, I won't be able to take Eli this weekend. I'd tell him myself, but —"

"Oh, *Reece* . . ."

The sweetness of her voice wrapped around him like a warm blanket, and much as he wanted to cling to it, Reece shrugged it off. He wanted what was best for her, and if that was Jimmy, well, so be it. He could wish her well and happiness without being witness to it. At least, he hoped he could.

"It isn't like Eli knew my dad, but . . ."

"But they spent some pretty amazing

hours together these past few weeks."

Okay. So Taylor got it. Got *him.* Well enough to read his mind, maybe even his heart, and know that Eli was facing yet another loss. Already.

"I'll give it a lot of thought and prayer before I explain things to him."

"I, ah, thanks, Taylor. I'd better get back to my mom. She's taking it pretty hard."

"How long have they been together?"

Have, he noted. How like her not to get all negative before she had to be. "Thirty-eight years."

"Wow. That's a lot of sharing."

Anyone else would have quoted the latest divorce statistics. Said his parents should be commended for outlasting most marriages. Leave it to Taylor to say the one thing that would put tears in his eyes and a sob in his throat.

What the heck was wrong with her? Didn't she realize this was hard enough without her being so . . . loving?

"I'm praying," she said, her voice even softer than a whisper, "for your dad and mom and for you, too."

"I, ah, thanks," he repeated.

"Can I say just one more thing before I let you go?"

He couldn't stop her, short of ending the

call. Didn't want to anyway, so . . . "Sure."

"What you think you saw . . ."

Now why'd she have to remind him of that ugly scene?

"Trust me, it wasn't what it looked like."

Oh. Really. So you, all tangled up in Jimmy's arms, kissin' the daylights out of him . . . that was a mirage, *huh?*

"Trust me," she echoed and hung up.

A flicker of hope flared in his heart as he stared at TAYLOR emblazoned across the tiny screen. For a reason he couldn't explain, he *did* trust her. The real question was . . . should she trust *him*?

Reece headed back to the ICU, where he intended to do some praying of his own. He didn't deserve the love of a woman like Taylor, but if the Good Lord answered his prayers, he'd spend the rest of his life earning it.

21

THREE YEARS LATER

"Hey, quit hoggin' the bowl," Reece said with a playful elbow nudge to Eli's ribs.

"Hey," he echoed, "it was your idea to stick me in the middle." And then he mimicked Stan Laurel's smile to a T.

Laughing, Taylor said, "These old movies are just as funny today as they were in the '40s."

Reece grabbed another handful of popcorn. "There are those who consider slapstick pedantic and silly."

"I'm sure glad we aren't *those.*"

Reece ruffled his hair. "That's m'boy."

Taylor went to the kitchen to refill their hot chocolate mugs.

"Will you bring me a napkin when you come back?" called Reece's mom.

"I'll be right there."

That's what she'd said that bleak Friday, nearly two weeks to the day when the ambulance had rushed his dad to the hospital. Before he could utter a syllable, she'd known, somehow, that he hadn't just called to cancel another weekend with Eli. "Oh, no," she'd said. "I'll be right there."

Not only had Taylor been at his side as his dad exhaled his last breath, but she'd helped him console his mom and make all the final arrangements for the wake, and the burial, and the small gathering of friends at Margo's house afterward.

And she'd been there ever since.

"Oh, cool," Eli said, pointing at the TV. "A commercial for Jimmy's movie."

"Such a handsome young man," Judith said. "And that voice. Mmm-mmm-mmm."

Eli clapped a hand over his eyes. "Sheesh, Grandmom, could you keep the mush to a minimum, please?"

Laughing, Judith said, "It's times like these I wish you weren't quite so bright, young man. Minimum, indeed!"

Reece watched as Jimmy raced from the right side of the screen to the left, dodging bullets from behind while firing a gleaming pistol over his shoulder. Hard to believe, Reece thought, that the singing movie star had once been boots over Stetson in love with his wife.

The thought raised a chuckle.

"What's so funny?" Eli wanted to know.

"Oh, nothing. Just thought of a joke I heard."

She came back into the room, carrying a tray of steaming mugs and a plate of her famous brownies. After delivering one of each to everyone, she flopped down beside Eli. "Best decision we ever made," she said, grabbing a treat, "was to take down that B&B sign. Don't get me wrong," she added, using the brownie as a pointer, "I loved meeting people from all over the country, but isn't it *nice,* just the four of us?"

"I like it better," Eli said.

"Me, too," his grandmother agreed.

"Well," Reece put in, "breakfast sure ain't the event it used to be."

Taylor reached behind Eli's head and smacked his shoulder. She'd done the same thing the night he'd gone to her house and made his big confession. No way he intended to give up on her without a fight, he'd told her before launching into the story of his pathetic life.

"You don't even know the *meaning* of the word self-centered," she'd announced, and proceeded to run down her own list: she'd forgotten to thank her mom for taking her to the ballet, forgotten to apologize to her dad on the morning of the big event; the next day, a tornado blew through town and crushed the church and everyone in it . . . including her parents. She'd deprived Mark of children by insisting they work hard and save money to buy a house first. And the *pièce de résistance,* ignoring the call her brother had placed, all the way from Afghanistan. She'd been too busy folding sheets and fluffing towels to pick up and found out later he'd called from the hospital tent to ask her to pray with him . . . on the very night he died.

After half an hour or so of playing Who's Baddest of Them All, she tired of the game and smacked his shoulder. "We might as well get married, then, because who else would have a couple of selfish, greedy, self-centered pigs like us?"

Reece reached behind Eli and mussed her hair. "Hey, remember the night you proposed to me?"

She groaned. "Will I *ever* hear the end of that?"

" 'Fraid not. You said 'for better or worse,' so . . ."

"Reece . . . really," his mother scolded. "You really should be more respectful of your wife."

Sometimes, he thought, *I wish Taylor hadn't insisted you move in with us.*

But that wasn't true, and he knew it. He loved having his mom in his life again. And Taylor had given him that, too.

Eli peeked under the quilt. "Say . . . what's going on under there?"

"It's just your baby brother," she said, "trying to prepare you for what's to come."

"Well, take it easy, or there will be popcorn and brownie crumbs all over the couch."

Callie chose that moment to hop onto Taylor's lap. "What's the matter," she cooed as the cat rubbed its face against her cheek, "you feelin' a bit left out of things?"

"Better watch it, fur-face," Reece said. "I took you out of that cat trap, I can put you back into it."

Callie took it as an invitation to leap over Eli and into Reece's lap.

So here he sat, master of the Misty Wolf Inn, surrounded by a live-in mother, an eight-year-old nephew-turned-son, a very pregnant wife, and a cat that was purring so loudly he was tempted to turn up the TV. *Long, long way from where you were before Taylor came into your life,* he thought, smiling to himself.

"I forget," Eli said, poking at the big white square in the middle of the quilt, "what's this one mean?"

"It means," she said, winking at Reece,

"there's room for me to add memories your brothers and sisters will make."

Reece winked back as Eli nodded.

"Oh yeah," he said. "That's right." He looked up at Taylor again to ask "Are you going to make memory quilts for all of them, too?"

"Well, maybe," she said, drawing out the word, "if there's time between all the cooking and baking and cleaning and —"

"Ugh," he teased. "Sorry I asked."

Now he stroked the square that had once been his fishing shirt and turned to Taylor. "Will you tell me the story of the quilt?"

"Again?"

Reece loved this game they played — Taylor pretending to hate the telling of it, Eli pretending it was the first time he'd heard the story of how each little scrap had become part of the quilt. And he had to admit, he liked hearing the story, too.

Taylor had turned the thing this way and that, reading all the captions, explaining how she'd assembled each patch, sewing by hand until her fingers were swollen and sore.

"Poor baby," Reece joked.

She pressed the back of her hand to her forehead. "Oh, yes," she sighed, "the things I've done . . ."

Eli grinned and bit his lips to keep from

blurting out the ending he'd heard so many times before. It was all Reece could do to keep from saying "Wait for it . . . wait for it . . ."

For a kid Eli's age, even one second was too long.

Winking, Reece lifted his hand to get Taylor and Judith's attention, and once he had it, he dropped it, like an orchestra conductor.

Their voices blended in discordant harmony that chased Callie from his lap:

". . . for love of Eli."

DISCUSSION QUESTIONS

1. What was Reece's most redeeming character trait?
2. What would you say is his least attractive personality quirk?
3. Is there one element to Taylor's personality that best defines her?
4. Is that element the reason you liked her?
5. Did you identify with any of her flaws?
6. And what about Reece? Do you feel that you have anything in common with him?
7. Who is your favorite secondary character?
8. Why does that individual stand out in your mind?
9. If you had to choose one spiritual theme for this story, what would it be?
10. If asked to describe the story in just a few sentences, what would you say about it?
11. Did you feel the interactions between main and secondary characters were realistic?

12. Without looking, can you remember the Bible verse that appeared on the first pages of this novel? (If you can, your memory is better than mine!)